MURDERER'S FETE

(first published as Feted To Die)

MURDERER'S FETE

an Inspector Constable murder mystery

by Roger Keevil

mail@rogerkeevil.co.uk

www.rogerkeevil.co.uk

Printed by CreateSpace, an Amazon.com company
Available on Kindle and other devices

To Christopher, my inspiration
'So great a cloud of witnesses'

*'Murderer's Fete' was first published in 2012 in paperback and as an e-book
under the title of 'Feted To Die'*

Chapter 1

"Dammett Hall."

"Who is it, darling?" floated a voice from the stairs.

"No, this is Seymour Cummings." A pause. "Hold on ... Sandra, it's Gideon Porter for you."

"On my way." Lady Lawdown swept into the drawing room. "Honestly, it isn't as if I didn't have enough to do today." She took the proffered handset. "Yes, Gideon, what can I do for you? ... Yes, the contractors finished putting it up yesterday evening, so it's all ready for you to bring everything up to the Hall tomorrow. ... Of course I have the licence here. My friends on the bench aren't likely to refuse a fellow J.P., are they? Now for goodness sake, stop fussing, Gideon. Just put your beer barrels on your little lorry, and we'll see you in the morning. Yes ... goodbye."

"What was that all about?"

"Oh, Seymour, with all your talents, don't tell me you can't guess."

"I shall treat that remark with the contempt it deserves."

"Sorry, darling, but I couldn't resist it. No, Gideon was flapping about the beer tent. I honestly have no idea why I put myself through this every year. It's wearing me to an absolute frazzle."

Lady Lawdown's appearance belied her words. A tall elegant woman in her fifties, with immaculate pale blonde hair and a perfect complexion enhanced with the subtlest make-up, long slim hands with beautifully manicured nails, and wearing a silk summer dress in a bold poppy print, she had the air of a duchess who expected royalty to drop in for tea at any moment, and who was not remotely fussed at the prospect.

Seymour Cummings laughed. "Sandra, you're a terrible liar and you know it. You absolutely love the annual fete - it gives you the perfect chance to queen it over the entire county, especially since Peter died. I shouldn't be at all surprised if that isn't why you married him in the first place."

"Seymour, that's a horrid thing to say," retorted Lady Lawdown. "I swear you make these things up just to annoy me.

I've a good mind to phone your editor and tell him that you're a complete fraud, and that you invent all those things you put in your column."

"Oh for heaven's sake, Sandra, I was only joking." Seymour sounded quite rattled. "Please don't do anything like that ..."

"Mummy, where are you?" came a voice from the hall.

"In here, darling."

Nobody seeing Laura Biding and Lady Lawdown together could doubt that they were mother and daughter. Mid-twenties, slightly shorter than her mother but with the same blonde colouring, Laura wore riding boots, jeans, and a t-shirt as if she belonged on the cover of a fashion magazine. On which, on one memorable occasion, she had appeared, as one of the featured subjects of a lead article about Daughters of the Aristocracy.

"I just wanted to let you know that Amelia Cook has arrived, Mummy. She's dropping some things off for tomorrow. I'm just going to unlock the kitchen door so she can bring all her food and equipment straight through. Now, is there anything else you need me to do?"

"Darling, you're an absolute treasure, isn't she, Seymour? I have no idea how on earth I'd manage if it weren't for you. She's done all the posters, and she's persuaded the Vicar to open the fete, and she's arranged all the attractions. Go on, darling - tell Seymour what you've organised."

Laura looked faintly embarrassed. "Honestly, Mummy, it really isn't anything special - mostly just the usual things, like the tombola and the white elephant stall and the children's races. Oh, and we've got Splat the Rat this year."

"Splat the Rat?" Seymour sounded baffled. "What on earth is that?"

"Oh, that one's great fun," explained Laura. "You have a length of drainpipe sloping down at an angle, and then the player waits at the bottom with an old cricket bat, and then you make a sort of big sausage out of rags and soak it in beer - that's the Rat - and you put it in the top of the pipe and the player tries to splat it as it comes out at the bottom."

"Hmm, I really must have a go at that," replied Seymour, not sounding totally convinced. "And speaking of rats, I dare say you've got Horace Cope coming yet again to put his two-pennyworth in."

"Oh please, Seymour, not again," pleaded Lady Lawdown.

Laura sat down next to Seymour on the sofa. "Now Seymour, please don't be horrid to Uncle Horace. You know he's always done the fortune-telling, ever since I can remember. It's a village tradition. And anyway, it's only a bit of harmless fun."

"The day Horace Cope becomes harmless is the day I give up the predicting business," snorted Seymour, "and goodness only knows when that will be. I just wish somebody would splat this particular rat."

"This is all because you're up against each other for the new TV show," said Lady Lawdown, "but I'm sure you don't really have anything to worry about. You're so much better on television than Horace. So can you please try not to upset him, just this once?"

"Yes, well, you don't know the whole story," replied Seymour.

"How do you mean? What's he done?"

Seymour waved a hand. "Don't worry about it, Sandra - it's nothing really. Look, as a favour to you, I'll try to be nice to him. Anyway, where are you putting him this year?"

"Laura had a brilliant idea for that. We've put his booth in the Secret Garden - you know, that little walled garden off the West Terrace. It's completely private so people can't crowd round and eavesdrop, and there's a gate in the wall which leads out into the Park, so we can keep it locked until the fete opens."

"And who is the old fool going to be this year?"

"Oh, now that was my idea." Lady Lawdown sounded quite pleased with herself. "He's going to be 'Swami Rami, Mystic Seer of the Future'. Isn't that a hoot?"

"Oh blast!" interjected Laura. "I haven't taken his sign round to the Park. I must do that, or nobody will be able to find him."

"Take it out through the side door," suggested Lady Lawdown. "No point in going all the way round. Do you want my gate key?"

"No, I'll take the one from the flower room."

"While you're at it, darling, do go round and check that it's all set up for Gideon at the beer tent. He phoned up just now, so I expect he'll come rushing up from the pub, and you'll probably have to hold his hand."

"Right, I'm off. And don't worry about a thing, Mummy. Everything is under control, and we're going to raise lots of lovely money."

"I do hope so, darling," replied Lady Lawdown with a slightly gloomy air. "I do hope so."

*

Although the entire village had been preparing for the annual Dammett Worthy Garden Fete for weeks, the day before the fete always saw the most hectic activity. If anything in Dammett Worthy could ever be called hectic.

Helen Highwater made her way from her cottage in Galley Alley towards the High Street for her usual morning coffee at the Copper Kettle Tearooms. Helen was an unremarkable-looking middle-aged woman with faded grey hair - to look at her, nobody would have suspected that she was one of Dammett Worthy's more celebrated residents, and probably the richest woman in the county. As the author of moderately successful children's books featuring badly-behaved field-mice having unexacting adventures on fairly dull farms, nobody could have been more surprised than Helen at the sudden and unexpected success of her story about a schoolgirl magician. But for some reason, 'Carrie Otter and the Photographer's Stain' had seized the imagination of a generation of children, and had led to a degree of fame, and a level of income, which had quite taken her breath away. The latest in the series, 'Carrie Otter and the Half-Boiled Pants', had even been nominated for both the Tomer Prize and the Brownbread Award, although not all the snootier critics approved of her populist style of writing, and some of the press had been downright dismissive. However, whenever anybody mentioned this to Helen, she gave her usual bright smile and shrugged off the comments. "Just wait until the last book comes out," she would say. "You can all make up your minds then." And the world did not have long to wait. The publicity machine for the launch of the final book in the series was in top gear for publication the following month.

Helen passed the premises of the local funeral directors, Solomon Binding (Undertaking), and turned in through the door of the Copper Kettle, just in time to see Amelia Cook disappearing through into the kitchen in a blur of flowered apron.

"Good morning, Amelia!" called Helen.

"Oh, morning, Helen. Be with you in a second, dear. Just getting a batch of scones out. There! Now, coffee and a cake, is it? I made a lovely Devil's Food Cake yesterday, and I gave the vicar a slice, and he said how nice it was, and then I told him what it was called, and the poor man nearly choked on it. So what do you think?"

"That would be lovely, Amelia."

"Well, you sit down by the window, dear, and I'll bring it over. Would you like the paper to look at? Oh, bother, I forgot - that dratted boy from the paper-shop missed me out this morning, and I haven't had a second to go over and get it. I've got yesterday's Evening Sin, if that's any good to you. You can read Horace's predictions for today. Oh, no, I forgot - you're not a big fan, are you?"

And in her usual flustered way which seemed completely at odds with her well-deserved reputation as the best cook for miles around, Amelia bustled about to bring Helen her order, and sat down in the chair opposite her.

"Are you all set for tomorrow?" she asked. "Ready to meet more of your adoring public?"

"Well, anything to help Sandra out a bit, I suppose," replied Helen, "although it's not really so much to sit at a table and sign books for an hour at a fiver a signature. But I do get nervous. Silly, isn't it? But you'll be up at the Hall as well, won't you? Didn't Sandra say you were doing the tea tent as usual?"

"Oh, don't remind me!" groaned Amelia. "Why on earth I say I'll do it I don't know. But there'll be nobody in the village tomorrow afternoon because they'll all be up at the fete, so I might as well close anyway. I can't move in my pantry for cakes already, and I've only got half of them done. And I'll have to finish everything at the last minute, or else things go stale. I wonder if I could get Mrs. Richards to help me after she's finished the cleaning at the Hall in the morning? Oh, I'm not looking forward to tomorrow. But, as you say, it's all for Sandra.

You can never say no to her, can you? It's the church roof this year, isn't it? Well, must get on. Maids of Honour next!"

And without waiting for a reply, Amelia darted back into the kitchen, leaving Helen to listen to the sound of rattling crockery as she gazed out of the window.

*

At Dunham Chambers, the offices of Messrs. Hall, Knight and Allday (Solicitors and Commissioners for Oaths) in Dammett Worthy High Street, Robin Allday was surveying the day's post.

Robin looked exactly what he was - a typical country solicitor. In his late forties, tall and lean, with horn-rimmed glasses and dark hair tending towards grey, he wore a slightly rumpled tweed suit and brown brogues as if born to the role. Among the usual heap of conveyancing documents, bills, and invitations to take out a selection of credit cards on advantageous terms, one item in particular appeared to hold his interest. He gazed at it for several minutes frowning, and then seemed to come to with a start, folded it and placed it in his jacket pocket, and with sudden resolution got to his feet.

"I'm just going over the road for a minute, Judith," he said to his secretary as he passed through the outer office. "I shan't be long."

"Yes, Mr. Allday," she replied in resigned tones. This was obviously nothing unusual.

Across the High Street stood the Dammett Well Inn, a long low timber-framed building decorated with hanging baskets overflowing with brightly-coloured plants. According to legend, the Inn had served as the village pub ever since King Richard III had stopped there on his way to the Battle of Bosworth to have a loose horseshoe repaired at the then village smithy, and had taken a tankard of ale while waiting. In view of the outcome of the battle, the landlord had decided against naming the inn 'The White Horse' after the king's charger, so it had been given the name of a local spring whose legendary magical powers were greatly prized by local maidens. Or those who claimed to be.

As Robin entered the lounge bar of the Dammett Well, he was greeted cheerfully by the landlord.

"Hallo, Robin. How are things? Don't usually see you in

here this early. Usual, is it?"

"Yes please, Gideon," said Robin. He sighed.

"Problems?"

"No, not really. Just all the usual rubbish about property titles not being clear and where the boundary is for such-and-such a field and people talking about changing their wills ..."

"None of which you're allowed to tell me about, and I wouldn't understand a word if you did," laughed Gideon. He was a round balding merry-looking man with spectacular mutton-chop whiskers and a ringing country burr, who gave the impression that he had taken over as landlord of the pub at some point in the Dickensian period and had somehow stuck in place. "Right, there's your brandy. I shouldn't fret too much about whatever-it-is if I were you, Robin. In my experience, there's very few things worth worrying yourself into an early grave for. Things always seem to sort themselves out. Here, I've just had a thought." He chuckled. "You could always go and get your fortune told up at the fete tomorrow. I suppose you're going?"

"I dare say," answered Robin with a wan smile. "Sandra's asked some of us up there for a drinks thing before it starts, so I expect I shall be there. Mind you, I'm not so sure about the fortune-telling business - it's Horace Cope again, as always, and he already knows far too much about everyone in the village as it is. And no doubt Albert will be there if there are free drinks involved ..."

"Heads up!" murmured Gideon in an undertone. "And a fine good morning to you, Mr. Ross. How are you this lovely day?"

"Very well, thank you, Gideon," replied the newcomer. "I just thought I'd pop in to say hello, and I saw Robin come in just now, so I thought, well, why not a quick one as I'm passing?"

"Why not indeed? So what can I get you?" enquired Gideon, with a wry sideways glance at Robin.

"No, let me get this, Albert," said Robin, opening his wallet. "G & T, isn't it? There, Gideon, you'd better take for both of them out of that."

"Well, that's extremely kind of you, Robin." Albert Ross was a small nondescript man with faded sandy hair whose age could have been anything between fifty and sixty-five. His

11

somewhat apologetic air was not improved by his habit of blinking at the world frequently and rapidly through thick round spectacles.

"Your cousin all set up for tomorrow then, Albert?" asked Gideon.

"Oh, Horace is always ready for anything," replied Albert. "He is so organised, he puts me to shame. Mind you, he has to be, with everything he has on his plate. He's just sent his latest book review off to The Sin on Sunday this morning, and when I came out he was starting to write the predictions for next week's papers, and then of course there's the new TV show, so when he gets that he'll be even busier."

"Now I heard a bit about that," said Gideon, "but I don't know the whole story, and I'm bound to get people asking because they all think I know everything round here. So what's it all about?"

"Well," said Albert, settling himself on a bar stool and taking a deep breath. "It's a new programme which is going to be on Satellite 5 every week, and it's called 'Seeing Stars'. It's a sort of magazine with celebrity guests telling their stories about supernatural experiences and how predictions came true for them and all that sort of thing, and they want to have as the presenter a really famous clairvoyant, who will also do his predictions for the coming week. And they've asked Horace if he would like to do it."

"Ah, now hang on," interrupted Gideon. "Didn't I hear that Seymour Cummings is also in line for the job?"

"I suppose he told you that himself," retorted Albert waspishly. "I wouldn't believe anything you hear from Seymour Cummings. No, Horace is the man, trust me. So he'll be up to London a lot more, won't he, Robin?"

"Er, yes, I suppose he will. Lord, look at the time. I have to go." And with that, Robin abruptly finished his drink, set down the glass, and hurried out, leaving the other two looking at each other in faint surprise at the suddenness of his departure.

Robin crossed the road and entered his office, where his secretary was just hanging up the phone.

"That was Mr. Palmer from Meadow Farm," she said. "He wanted an appointment, so I've told him he can come on

Wednesday at eleven o'clock."

"Well, he can't," replied Robin shortly. "You'll have to ring him back and make it another day. And if there's anything else for Wednesday, cancel it."

He entered his office and, quietly but firmly, closed the door.

*

Ivor Pugh surveyed the view from the top of the church tower with a gentle smile. In the far distance, rolling hills studded with beech woods were interleaved with green pasture and the striking yellow of oilseed rape. Closer, within the tree-lined curve of the unseen river, the chimneys of Dammett Hall rose above the solitary gigantic cedar which dominated the front lawns where tents were already appearing for the next day's fete. And clustered around the feet of the church, Dammett Worthy itself, a collection of tile, thatch and slate punctuated by the multicoloured patchwork of the supermarket car park.

Ever since becoming vicar at the parish church of St. Salyve some twenty-seven years earlier, the Reverend Pugh had always tried to find a few moments every day to climb the tower and look out over his parish. He felt that, in a sense, it brought him closer to his flock and closer to God at the same time. Having recovered his breath, for the hundred and sixty-eight steeply-winding steps never seemed to get any easier to climb, he started down again, passing the bell chamber and the ringing room where the ropes hung expectantly, before emerging next to the vestry door at the foot of the tower. A sudden thought struck him, and he approached the altar to check the water in the flanking flower arrangements. No, all was well - the Flower Society had not been so pre-occupied with preparations for the fete that they had neglected their duties in the church.

The vicar was a short grey-haired man whose sprightly walk and perky manner belied his seventy-four years, and were reminiscent of nothing more than a robin alighting on a bird-table in search of breakfast. Humming 'Onward Christian Soldiers' under his breath, he made his way along the nave towards the west door which opened abruptly in his face, causing him to jump back with a surprised cry of "Good Lord!".

13

"Sorry to disappoint you, vicar," came the reply. "Only me, I'm afraid. Did I make you jump?"

"Well, yes, you did, as a matter of fact," answered the vicar slightly breathlessly. "But no matter. Were you looking for me, Mr. Cope?"

"Horace, please, vicar, otherwise I shall have to call you Reverend Pugh, and that sounds so formal and unfriendly," responded his visitor in an arch voice. "And we can't have that, can we? All friends together, that's what we are in our little village - am I right?"

Horace Cope gave what he obviously thought was a winning smile. The effect was not quite what he hoped. His round shiny face, perched atop a short plump body clad in a check suit in shades of fawn and green, was crowned by strands of greasy hair drawn across a bald crown, giving him the look of a disreputable bookmaker about to explain why he could not pay out a bet.

"Yes, of course, Mr. Cope ... er ... Horace. Now," continued the vicar, in tones in which only a close observer could have detected the faintest hint of irritation, "What did you want me for?"

"It wasn't really you I was wanting, actually," replied Horace. "I was out for a stroll round the village, and as I came past the churchyard I thought I'd have my usual few minutes at the Dammett Well ... my little 'communion with the spirits', as I call it ..."

"Hmmm, quite!" The irritation in the Reverend Pugh's voice grew plainer.

"Sorry, vicar, no offence intended." Horace did not sound remotely contrite. "But I thought that with my little fortune-telling performance coming up at the fete tomorrow, I might as well enlist all the help I can get." He giggled. "And then I thought, while I'm here, why not have another little burrow through your church registers, if that's all right by you. You never know that reminding myself of the name of some village girl's granny may come in useful. You know what I always say - the Well for inspiration, the Church for information!"

The vicar sighed. "Yes, er ... Horace. Of course you may look at the registers again. As they are public documents, you have every right." The word 'unfortunately' remained

14

unspoken. "You know where they are. Please make sure you put them back in the cupboard when you've finished. And now, if you'll excuse me, I have to go out. Her Ladyship is expecting me up at the Hall to confirm some arrangements for the fete."

"Oh yes, of course, you're opening it, aren't you? How lovely!" cried Horace. "No doubt I shall see you up there beforehand - you will be at Sandra's do for a little drinkie first to steady the nerves, won't you? Well, you mustn't keep the Lady waiting. I'll see you tomorrow at twelve. Toodle-pip!"

And with a gay wave of his hand, Horace disappeared into the vestry. Ivor Pugh stepped out into the churchyard, took a deep breath of fresh air, and started down the path towards the lychgate.

Chapter 2

A brisk breeze was snapping the flag flying from the roof of Dammett Hall, but it could not totally dispel the warmth of a beautiful summer's day. All morning the south lawn had seen a constant buzz of activity, as a procession of cars disgorged flower arrangements, cages of guinea-pigs, folding wooden chairs, bunches of enormous carrots, wedding cakes, wrought-iron boot-scrapers, and the thousand other things which go to make up a traditional fete in the English countryside. Visibly in charge and glowing with enthusiasm, Laura Biding with clipboard in hand seemed to be everywhere at once, pointing new arrivals towards the correct tent, rounding up toddlers who had escaped from the car while their mothers were unloading the boot, instructing the Scouts on the programme of sports events, and all with an air of calm competence which seemed to indicate that nothing had been left to chance.

Lady Lawdown looked out of the drawing room window at the preparations in hand and smiled fondly. A knock came at the door, and Amelia Cook entered carrying a tray.

"I thought you might like some coffee, Your Ladyship."

"Oh, Amelia, you're so thoughtful. Thank you so much. I haven't had a moment to think about anything, and I expect you're rushed off your feet in the kitchen. What a shame Mrs. Richards couldn't stay to help, but I dare say you've got it all under control. You wouldn't mind just popping up to Mr. Cummings' room and telling him there's coffee waiting, would you? Lovely."

A few minutes later, Seymour Cummings entered the room. His fifty-odd years sat easily on him alongside a healthy tan, and he wore his comfortably casual check shirt and cord trousers as if born to the country lifestyle, yet with a touch of sleekness which hinted at a level of city sophistication and the money that went with it. He joined Lady Lawdown at her vantage point at the window and looked out over the preparations taking place on the lawns.

"Morning, Sandra," he said, greeting her with a peck on the cheek. "Laura seems to be on top of everything. I feel I should offer to help, but I'm feeling awfully lazy this morning. I hope you didn't mind me not coming down for breakfast."

"Of course I didn't, darling," replied Lady Lawdown, "although Mrs. Richards was rather sniffy. You know she likes to do the whole country-house-breakfast thing when I have someone staying. But I told her that you were probably still quite exhausted from your lecture tour, and you deserved a lie-in on your first Saturday. Just autograph your column in tomorrow's Sunday Stir for her in the morning - that will brighten her up. Anyway, do have some of this coffee Amelia's made for us, or you'll be in her bad books too."

"Amelia's far too busy to worry about me," smiled Seymour, pouring coffee. "The last time I saw her, she was scampering back downstairs to carry on in the kitchen. Something about critical timing on a batch of quiches. Now sit back and drink this. Brandy?"

"Oh lord, no, darling. I'd better not start just yet. I shall be on the alcohol soon enough. You haven't forgotten that I've got people coming for drinks before the fete, have you?"

"Actually, I had," groaned Seymour. "I thought you invited me down here to rest my weary bones, not to stand in as your social host."

"Don't be silly, Seymour," laughed Lady Lawdown. "It's just a few friends. Helen's coming, and Robin Allday, and the vicar has to be here because he's opening the fete. Then there's Albert Ross and, of course, Horace." And as Seymour opened his mouth in protest, she swiftly forestalled him. "Don't forget what you promised, darling. No unpleasantness."

"Oh very well," sighed Seymour. "Anyway, what time are they coming?"

"I said about mid-day."

"Then we still have three-quarters of an hour. You can sit back and think beautiful thoughts. I think I'll pop out for a stroll round to offer Laura a bit of moral support. Just as long as she doesn't rope me into anything strenuous."

*

"Hello, Sandra! Only me!" Helen Highwater's voice echoed up the staircase of Dammett Hall. "I hope I'm not too early."

Sandra Lawdown appeared framed in the arch at the top

of the stairs. The pose was only slightly self-conscious, and the graceful descent would have done credit to a top model.

"Helen, dear, not at all. You know you're welcome any time. It's only just coming up to twelve. Do come on through." And she led the way into the drawing room. "Right, let's have a little something - we can get a head start on the others. I have a feeling I'm going to need a few drinks to get through today. Sherry as usual, is it?"

"Lovely, thank you. You're not worried about this afternoon, are you? The fete seems all under control, from what I could see coming up the drive. I'm sure Laura's on top of everything - well, she always is, every year. That girl's a marvel. How she does it I don't know."

"Oh, it's not the fete, darling," replied Lady Lawdown. "That always runs like clockwork. No, it's the people. You talk about Laura. I know there's something at the back of her mind that's bothering her. She seems quite calm and organised, but I'm sure there's something ... a mother always knows."

"Laura? Oh surely not. Perhaps she's in love," smiled Helen. "Hasn't she been seen around with Robin Allday quite a lot lately? Now there's a lovely man. And he's always so helpful."

"I can't imagine she's interested in Robin," retorted Lady Lawdown dismissively, pouring herself a brandy. "He's a charming man and we both like him very much, but I can't see Laura going for a middle-aged man. I should have thought she was far more likely to be involved with somebody from her London set."

"Any news of any more work in that line?"

"Not that I know of. She goes up to London for auditions and photographic sessions every so often, but nothing ever seems to come of it. I don't think her agent can be very good. She doesn't really talk that much about it."

"Well, perhaps that's what's on her mind," suggested Helen. "She feels she isn't contributing to the household because she's short of money."

"She has her allowance from the trust which Peter left her," responded Lady Lawdown, "which was very generous, considering he was under no obligation to do so. Oh, for heaven's sake, let's talk about something other than money. It only reminds me about the blasted Hall roof! Wouldn't it be nice if we could have all of today's cash to have that fixed, instead of half of it going to the church?"

At that moment, the sound of the front door slamming was heard from the hall, and Laura Biding appeared in the drawing room doorway.

"Right, I hope that's everything," she sighed, subsiding on to a sofa. "I'm shattered, but I think everybody knows what they're doing - all the stalls are ready and waiting, there's already a queue at the gates, and I've just seen the vicar coming up the drive. I deserve a drink!"

"Darling, what on earth would I do without you? What would you like?"

"A very large scotch, please, Mummy. Then I can breathe booze all over the vicar and scandalise him!" She laughed.

"Would you like me to pop out and watch for him?" asked Helen. "You know he'll only dither about on the steps otherwise."

"Would you, dear?" said Lady Lawdown, and Helen disappeared into the hall as a clock at the foot of the stairs began to strike the hour.

"Where's Seymour?" enquired Laura. "I thought he would have been first to the whisky. Don't tell me he's abandoned you."

"He's gone for a walk, darling. I'm surprised you haven't seen him - he said he was going to come and give you some moral support."

"Fat chance!" snorted Laura.

Voices were heard from the hall, and Helen ushered Ivor Pugh into the drawing room. The vicar's round face was a little pinker than usual under his panama hat, and he was perspiring slightly.

"Good morning, your ladyship. Oh no, I tell a lie, it's good afternoon! Do forgive me, but I'm a bit puffed. Gracious me, that drive of yours never seems to get any shorter, does it? Do you mind if I sit down?" And he subsided on to the sofa next to Laura.

"What you need, Mr. Pugh, is a drink to set you up," replied Lady Lawdown. "I can't have you collapsing on the job when we can't start the fete without you. What's your poison?"

19

"Just the tiniest whisky would be very welcome, thank you ... well, just a little more, if I may. Oh, thank you so much, your ladyship. Well, haven't we got a lovely day for it? It looks as if all your hard work has paid off, Laura. And you're looking as lovely as ever, if I may say so, my dear."

"You're very sweet, vicar," smiled Laura. "But I can't take all the credit for today. Are you sure you haven't been putting in a word with your friend upstairs to arrange some good weather for us?"

"Laura!" Lady Lawdown sounded shocked. "What a thing to say!"

"Oh please don't worry, your ladyship," twinkled the vicar. "No offence taken, I assure you. It just goes to show that Laura is still the same naughty little girl at heart as when she first came to the Hall ... what is it, fifteen years ago? Just when you married his lordship. I really do think Laura was one of the prettiest bridesmaids I've ever seen. Another? Well, I suppose the weeniest drop more won't do any harm, will it?"

The distant tinkling of a bell was heard from the servants' quarters at that moment, together with the sound of the front door opening.

"Yoo hoo! Anyone there? It's only us chickens!"

"Horace!" grunted Helen. "I was wondering when he would put in an appearance!" And as Laura made to get up, "No, stay where you are, Laura. I'll go." A door was heard to open. "It's all right, Amelia, I'm on my way," called Helen towards the kitchen as she entered the hall. "Horace ... and you've brought Albert with you. How nice! We're in here." She led the way into the drawing room.

Horace Cope's smiling face seemed even shinier than ever, an impression accentuated by a flamboyant scarlet floppy-collared shirt accompanied by a large gold medallion on a chain around his neck. A light-blue linen jacket was draped around his shoulders with artful casualness. Behind him, Albert Ross was a complete contrast, drab in beige trousers and a fawn pullover, and carrying a large suitcase which he dropped with a sigh of relief.

"Good grief, Uncle Horace," laughed Laura. "Where on earth did you get that shirt? You look like a refugee from the 1970s!"

"I can't imagine how you would know that, Laura!" replied Horace. "You're far too young. No, it's just a little costume to help with my character. You know I like to give a good performance. I have some big red curly-toed slippers, and just you wait until you see my robe - it's turquoise and gold, and there's an enormous matching turban. And Albert is going to do some make-up for me and give me lovely big eyebrows."

"I can hardly wait," commented Lady Lawdown drily.

"Well, you won't have to wait for long, Sandra, will you? Just come and have a little chat with me in my tent, and I'll tell you your future. No charge! Goodness, where are my manners? These are for you." And Horace handed over the extravagantly-beribboned bouquet of lilies he carried.

"Horace, how sweet," exclaimed Lady Lawdown. "Aren't you generous? They're beautiful."

"I hope you don't mind lilies," remarked Horace. "Some people say they put them in mind of death, but I think that's just superstitious nonsense. That reminds me, Helen, I hope you're ready for all those adoring fans of yours. They can't get enough, can they? Bet they'll be quizzing you about the new book. Well, isn't this lovely? It's quite a party, isn't it."

"Then you'd better have a drink, hadn't you," replied Lady Lawdown.

"Just a very quick sherry, and then I absolutely must get on. No, don't move - Albert will do it, if that's all right with you. I don't want to break up this lovely picture." He surveyed the gathering with an approving smile. "It's too perfect - really, it's too good to be true. The Lady of the Manor in all her glory - her beautiful daughter, as pretty as a picture - Helen, one of our village's most celebrated successes with those marvellous surprising books of hers - the Reverend Pugh, the moral guiding light of the community. Thank you so much, Albert." He took the proffered glass and sipped. "I simply can't imagine what it would be like if you weren't around to look after me." He grinned toothily. "But where's our resident legal eagle? I thought Robin Allday would be here as well to keep us all on the straight and narrow. Perhaps he's been detained. Oh, I do hope not. We can't have the Church without the Law, if you don't mind my little joke, vicar! And of course, Sandra, you have dear Seymour staying with you. Surely he will be gracing us with his presence. Or has something unforeseen cropped up to keep him away?" He chuckled.

"I'm sure both Robin and Seymour are about somewhere," said Lady Lawdown. "Well, Horace, we mustn't keep you. I expect you have lots to do to get ready."

"I do," responded Horace, downing the last of his sherry. "Come along, Albert. Bring my things."

"Oh, surely you can manage without Albert for five minutes," put in Helen.

"Of course you can," agreed Laura. "Poor Albert hasn't even had a drink yet. We'll send him through in a minute. You know your way to the Secret Garden, don't you - the flower room door is unlocked, and your booth is all set up ready. Albert drinks G & T, Mummy."

"Oh ... very well," assented Horace, a touch grumpily. "I shall see you in a moment, then, Albert." And picking up the case, he left the room.

*

Lady Lawdown occupied herself pouring Albert Ross a drink.

"He knows," she thought. "Where does that leave me? Oh, what on earth am I going to do?"

Robin Allday sat at his desk with his head in his hands.

"He knows," he thought. "I'm finished. Where the hell did he get the information?"

Laura Biding glanced out of the window at the busy villagers of Dammett Worthy putting the final touches to the fete.

"He knows," she thought. "How can I ever look anybody in the face again?"

Seymour Cummings leaned against a tree, lit a cigarette, and sighed.

"He knows," he thought. "I don't know what possessed me to do it. Well, that puts an end to that."

Helen Highwater realised she was gazing unfocussed into space, and put a bright smile on her face.

"He knows," she thought. "Why can't you trust anybody these days? I don't suppose there's a thing I can do about it."

Albert Ross took his glass and tentatively sat in a chair by the fireplace.

"He knows," he thought. "And I thought I'd been so clever. I just wish I could find a way to change his mind."

*

"So, Albert," said Lady Lawdown, "what have you been up to lately?"

"Oh ... um ... well, not a great deal, really. I've been doing some bits and pieces for Horace around the garden at Crystal Cottage, and of course I look after the house for him whenever he's away and keep it neat and tidy."

"So he's using you as some sort of unpaid housekeeper, is he?" asked Helen. "Isn't that Horace all over? Mind you, he'd never get anyone to come in and clean for him, with the amount of knick-knacks he's got cluttering up the place. He must be quite relieved he's got you."

"Honestly, Helen, I really think it's the least I can do, considering. And some of the things in Horace's collections are quite beautiful and very precious - I feel quite lucky that he trusts me to look after them. I'm just very grateful that he's let me stay there so long."

"No sign of anything on the horizon?" enquired Lady Lawdown delicately.

"What ...oh, you mean a job. No, not at the moment." Albert shook his head sadly. "I'm sure something will turn up."

"Don't worry, Albert," said Laura robustly. "You're no more skint than the rest of us, I expect. Well, except for you, Helen, and you haven't got a care in the world. Anyway, Albert, do tell ... what's in that great big case you lugged in here?"

"Oh, that's all Horace's props - he's brought the whole lot, you know. Well, he didn't have to carry them, did he? There's his crystal ball, which weighs a ton on its own, and then he's got packs of tarot cards, and a set of runes, and goodness knows what else besides. Joss sticks and incense cones for atmosphere. And there's the costume he was telling you about - that's come on hire from London, you know - and his box of make-up. Heavens!" he ejaculated, leaping to his feet. "The make-up! I promised to do it. Horace will be wondering where I am. I'd better go. Thank you for the drink." He rushed to the door.

"Out through the flower room is quickest," advised Laura.

23

"Yes, I know the way. Thank you. I'll see you later." His voice died away.

"Poor man," said Helen. "I do feel Horace puts upon him. Anyway, enough about them. Vicar, do cheer us up. Let's have some good news."

"Yes, Mr. Pugh," smiled Laura. "There must be some village gossip you can tell us. Have another drink and give us the latest from the Women's Institute."

"Now you know I don't approve of gossip, Laura. Although I heard there was a suggestion that the ladies might raise some money by doing a naked calendar," replied the vicar, turning pinker, "but I don't really think that's the sort of thing we want to see in Dammett Worthy, is it? Actually, I'm not absolutely sure that it was a serious proposal. Isn't that rather passé these days? I do think some of the younger members of my congregation like to tease me sometimes. I suppose it's my age. I really ought to be grateful that I have any younger congregation members at all, considering the state of some country parishes."

"Now vicar, you know we all think you're absolutely sweet. Especially the Brownies ... not to mention some of their mothers." The vicar's blush grew deeper.

"Laura, stop it!" said Lady Lawdown. "You are a worse tease than anybody!"

"Don't worry, your ladyship," responded the vicar. "I'm not such an old fogey that I can't enjoy Laura's little joke. But that reminds me. If you don't mind, your ladyship, I shall just pop outside and have a word with Brown Owl about the Brownies' painting competition. I certainly don't want a repetition of last year."

"Why, what happened last year?" asked Helen.

"There was a most unseemly brawl between two of the mothers when the results were announced. I seem to recall some mention of doping. I really can't have that again. Some of the language was verging on the profane, and it's not at all a good example for the little ones, is it? So if you'll excuse me ..."

"Yes, of course, vicar," replied Lady Lawdown, "but don't forget to come back, will you? We can't very well start without you."

"I shall be two ticks, never fear."

"Do you want me to come with you to keep order?" enquired Laura.

"No need, my dear," the vicar reassured her. "Take the chance to put your feet up for a minute. I'm sure you haven't stopped all morning. Go on, have another little drink. Be a devil!" And with an unexpectedly boyish chuckle, he made for the hall, where a few seconds later the front door closed behind him.

"D'you know, that's exactly what I'm going to do," said Laura, getting to her feet and heading for the drinks table.

"I don't think so, darling," commented Lady Lawdown. "Between the two of you, you and Mr. Pugh have practically finished the bottle."

"Well, I shall have to go and get another one, shan't I?" replied Laura practically. "I assume we have some more in the butler's pantry, unless Seymour's been towsing it on the sly. Shan't be a minute. Oh, do you think I ought to go and change out of jeans for the opening?"

"Of course not, Laura," said Helen. "You look lovely as you are. I'll come with you - I expect you could do with a hand. And you really ought to put those flowers in a vase, Sandra. Would you like one from the flower room?"

"You are thoughtful, Helen dear." And as the other two left the drawing room, Lady Lawdown crossed to the window again and gazed out over the grounds of Dammett Hall. She had never grown tired of the view across the park dotted with oaks, with the magnificent cedar tree in the foreground and the long slope down to the rush-fringed lake. And now it was all at risk. Her lip quivered, and she surreptitiously wiped away a tear. She felt very alone.

*

"Seymour, where on earth have you been hiding yourself?" As Laura Biding emerged from the library, she almost collided with Seymour Cummings and Albert Ross at the foot of the stairs. "We've all been wondering where you were. I thought I might have to send out a search party!"

"The only thing I'm in search of at the moment is a drink. Which," he observed, indicating the bottle which Laura carried, "you seem perfectly equipped to provide. So lead the way, my dear. Come along, Albert - let's go and get a quick one in before

25

all the ghastly jollity begins."

"Look who I've found skulking in the hall, Mummy," declared Laura, as she opened the drawing room door to reveal Lady Lawdown pacing restlessly in front of the fireplace. "He claims he's looking for a drink."

"Oh Seymour, there you are," said Sandra Lawdown, looking round with what seemed like relief. "I wish you'd been here earlier."

"Dreadfully sorry, ma'am," smiled Seymour. "I have to admit to going absent without leave. Why, have I missed something exciting?"

"No, not at all. It's just that ... well, when I have visitors, it's more pleasant if my house guest is here to help me entertain them."

"To tell you the honest truth, Sandra, that was my main reason for doing the disappearing act. I didn't really trust myself to keep my promise to be nice to Horace. Sorry, Albert, no offence, but you know he and I ... well, enough said."

"Ah, Seymour. They've found you at last!" Helen Highwater came in from the hall, closing the door behind her.

"Please don't you give me a hard time as well," groaned Seymour, "otherwise I really shall go and hide. Anyway, I don't appear to be the only one missing. I thought you were expecting Robin Allday as well."

"He's on his way," said Laura quickly. "I've just phoned him. Now, let me do these drinks. Helen?"

"Not for me, dear. I need to be able to hold a pen, and I'm shaking enough as it is. I don't know why, but these book signings always make me so nervous. I'll just have a glass of water - yes, soda water's fine."

"Seymour? No need to ask." She smiled. "One scotch coming up, and I shan't bother to get you to say when, because I know you won't. Right, there's yours. Albert?"

"Albert will have a large gin and tonic as usual," put in Seymour. "Plenty of gin, not much tonic, and no ice. Isn't that right, Albert?"

"Well, yes, as a matter of fact it is, Seymour. But how ..."

"I ought to know by now. I've seen you drink enough of them in the Dammett Well. Paid for most of them too," he commented in a not-particularly-successful undertone to Laura.

"Mummy?"

"I'll have just a little something to settle my nerves, darling. I'll have a brandy."

*

"Sandra, I don't suppose I'm still in time for that drink you invited me for?"

The door had opened, and Robin Allday stood on the threshold.

"Robin, I'm so glad you've made it," exclaimed Lady Lawdown with evident pleasure. "We'd almost given up on you."

"Never! Sorry I'm so late, but you know how things are in the law - there's always something unexpected," replied Robin. "Thank you, Laura. Well, cheers, everybody. Are we all set up for this afternoon?"

"If we aren't now, we never shall be!" remarked Laura. "Ah, here's the vicar back. Come on in, Mr. Pugh. We're just having a final drink before the off. Come along - there's another wee drop of whisky for you to lift your spirits. Are you all ready with your speech?"

"Hardly a speech, Laura. Just a few I hope well-chosen words. Nobody wants a sermon today."

"Indeed they don't," commented Seymour feelingly.

"Hell and damnation!"

"What is it, darling?" asked Lady Lawdown.

"The gate to the Secret Garden," answered Laura. "I've forgotten to unlock it. Nobody will be able to get in from the Park to have their fortune told. I'd better go and do it now."

"No, darling. You stay here - I'm sure Mr. Pugh wouldn't mind doing it. Here, vicar, take my keys." She took a bunch from her handbag on a small bureau by the fireplace. "It's that little one there. If you just pop out through the flower room and turn left, the gate is just the other side of Horace's tent. And if you could just check with him to make sure he's ready. That's if you don't mind ..."

"Not at all, your ladyship. I shall be two shakes of a lamb's tail. And then we shall be ... what is it they say ... all systems go." He hurried from the room.

*

It seemed only moments later that the vicar stood in the

27

drawing room doorway again. His face was no longer pink, and bore an expression of shock.

"What is it?" asked Lady Lawdown. "Is everything all right?"

"No, your ladyship. No, it isn't. Not at all. Oh dear! Oh my goodness!"

"Come on, man," said Seymour. "For goodness sake, tell us."

"It's Horace Cope. He's ... he's ..." The vicar's eyes turned upwards, and he crumpled to the floor.

Chapter 3

"Guv!"

Detective Inspector Andy Constable looked up from the heap of documents on his desk. In his forties, standing an unthreatening six feet tall, he carried only a little more weight than he should, and had a habit of pushing his iron-grey hair away from his friendly brown eyes, eyes which easily encouraged confidences from witnesses, but which could turn frighteningly icy, as many criminals could testify.

He looked relieved at the interruption. If he was honest with himself, he had never been particularly at home with paperwork, and the current official pre-occupation with forms, monitoring, and targets left him cold. Ever since he had joined the force some twenty-odd years before, he had always thought of himself as more of an instinctive rather than a by-the-book policeman, and although that had raised many an eyebrow during his career, it didn't seem to have stood in his way when promotions came around. And after the first two or three years, even the jokes about his surname had faded away. As for his first name, he intended to make sure the problem never arose. His colleagues liked him - there was something refreshingly no-nonsense about Andy - and his subordinates respected and trusted him. From some of the off-record remarks about the upper ranks which he occasionally overheard drifting down the stairwell at the station, that was rarer than his superiors would have wished.

"Yes, sergeant?"

"We've got a body, sir."

"Ah, now that's just what I needed."

"Sir?"

"Some proper police work to take me away from all this mumbo-jumbo. I take it there are suspicious circumstances?"

"Sounds like it to me, sir."

"Well, don't hover about in the doorway. Come in and tell me all about it."

Detective Sergeant Dave Copper came in and sat alongside the desk. Shorter than his superior and almost twenty years younger, he could never shake off the impression in others that he was stricken with a form of hero-worship for the older man. His air of being a slightly-undisciplined puppy caused occasional smiles among some other officers at the station, but nobody ever failed to be impressed by the dramatic turn of speed he could muster up when the need arose. He was, in fact, almost a legend for the number of joyriders, abandoning their stolen vehicles on one of the town's several council estates, he had managed to chase down. He had worked with Andy Constable for three years before being promoted to sergeant recently, and the two were regularly referred to in the canteen as AC/DC. But never in their hearing. So far.

"It's the fete at Dammett Hall."

"Whose fate?" Inspector Constable was momentarily puzzled.

"No sir, the Dammett Worthy Garden Fete. They hold it at Dammett Hall every year. It was just about to open when they discovered some bloke dead."

"Some bloke dead ...? Now that's what I like about you, sergeant - your ability to cut straight to the technical aspects of a case. Right, I suppose we'd better get over there and find out what it's all about." He stood and reached for his jacket. "Any idea why I'm the lucky man who gets a reprieve from all this pile of guff?" He gestured to his desk.

"Apparently you were asked for specially, sir."

"Why should the brass want me in particular?" Constable wanted to know.

"Not them, sir. It was the lady."

"What lady?"

"Lady Lawdown, sir. J.P. , sir."

"Oh fabulous! The chairman of the bench of magistrates. Oh bloody hell! Why me?"

"I understand that you've impressed the lady when she's seen you in court, sir. That's the word from upstairs, anyway. But I'm just the messenger boy."

"Copper, if that smirk stays on your face one second longer, you'll find yourself on traffic duty on market day for the next six months. Get the car. You're driving."

*

Once past Dammett Worthy, the road was lined with a

sporadic straggle of families heading towards the village. At the gates of Dammett Hall, a small crowd stood around a sign boldly proclaiming 'Today! Dammett Worthy Garden Fete', to which was sellotaped a hastily-improvised 'Cancelled', and the local constable had parked his car and taken up his post in the middle of the gateway to deter those villagers who doubted the truth of the statement.

"Doctor's up there already, sir," he replied in response to Inspector Constable's enquiry, and waved them through.

As the car turned the last corner of the drive, Dammett Hall emerged from behind a screen of trees. The house was a gem, small but perfect. Set on a low platform, two storeys of soft red bricks contrasted with the creamy grey of the stones at the corners and around the front door, with three discreet dormer windows and a cluster of surprisingly tall chimneys adding interest to the roof. Colonnades backed with blind brick walls flanked the house. To the right stretched the lawns which fell towards the lake. To the left stood a ghost village of marquees and stalls, eerily empty of activity.

"Now that," said Dave Copper appreciatively, "is what you call a very nice bit of real estate."

"You could say that," responded the inspector. "The lady's done very well for herself, hasn't she?"

"Not the old ancestral home, then?" enquired Copper.

"The Lawdown family, yes. They've been here for centuries. But of course, her ladyship's only a Lawdown by marriage, isn't she? Not actually landed gentry herself, although you'd never know it to look at her. As you are about to find out."

Sergeant Copper drove the car to the foot of the steps of the front door, parking between a small smart open-top sports car and the police doctor's rather grubby Volvo estate, as an attractive young woman emerged from the Hall to greet them.

"Good afternoon. Inspector ... Constable, isn't it? How do you do?" She shook hands.

"Good afternoon, Miss. This is Sergeant Copper." The two officers proffered their warrant cards. "And you are ...?"

"Sorry, Inspector, I should have said. We're all a bit upside down at the moment. My name's Laura Biding - I'm Lady Lawdown's daughter. You'd better come inside."

"Your car, miss?" enquired Copper, with envious eyes on

31

the sports car.

"Yes, sergeant," said Laura. "Why, will it be in the way there?"

"Not at all, miss."

Laura led the way through the door into a lofty hall painted in muted shades of grey and cream, into which afternoon sunlight streamed from a central domed skylight. Doors opened to left and right, and an elegant staircase led to the floor above. The Lawdowns of former generations looked down on the visitors.

"So, Inspector, what would you like to do first?" asked Laura. "Do you want to see ... where it happened ... or do you want to talk to people? Everybody's in here in the drawing room."

"I think we'd better find out exactly what's happened first, miss, if you could show us the way."

"Yes, of course. It's through here." Laura turned to the left through a green baize door which led into a short corridor, at the end of which the officers passed through a small room containing shelves, a sink, and a clutter of wellington boots, raincoats, watering cans, vases and flowerpots, and then out on to a paved terrace. Through an arch and down a flight of stone steps, the group emerged into a small enclosed garden, surrounded on all sides by brick walls covered with a selection of roses, honeysuckles, and other climbing plants. There was a discreet wooden door in the wall to the left, which appeared to lead in the direction of the main grounds. Low box hedges surrounded minute flowerbeds and a tiny central lawn, on which was pitched an incongruously-garish striped canvas tent, through whose entrance a plump jolly-looking man was just emerging.

"Beaten you to it again, Andy!" he cried. "You really are going to have to be quicker off the mark!"

"And good afternoon to you too, Doctor," smiled Constable. "It never ceases to amaze me how a spot of violent death always puts you in a good mood. I take it we do have a violent death, otherwise what are we doing here?"

"Oh, this one's a beauty," replied the doctor. "I've never seen one like this before. Do you want to come and have a look?"

"Inspector, do you really need me for this?" interposed Laura.

"No, of course not, Miss Biding," said Constable. "Sorry, I should have thought. Copper, would you take the young lady indoors to join the others. Ask them to stay put for the moment, and then come back out here."

"Righty-ho, guv. After you, miss." Laura Biding and Sergeant Copper disappeared through the arch towards the house.

"I am going to have to stop Copper reading cheap 1930s detective stories," sighed the inspector. "He is beginning to sound like a cliché sidekick. Anyway, who have we got?"

"Local man by the name of Horace Cope," responded the doctor. "Something of a celebrity, I gather."

Inspector Constable groaned. "We all know what that means. Trouble. What sort of celebrity? I've never heard of him."

"That," replied the doctor smugly, "is because you read the wrong sort of papers. He's a bit of an odd mix - well, was. He's a clairvoyant."

"You're kidding!"

"Have you ever known me to joke, inspector?" chuckled the doctor. "I'm surprised you don't know the name, because he crops up on TV from time to time. I think he's even done some work for the Met when they've been having one of their more touchy-feely alternative-methods moments. Load of rubbish, of course - never any scientific basis. And he's got a 'Your Stars' column in the Evening Sin - you know the usual tosh about journeys over water and tall dark strangers. I never read them myself."

"No, of course not," smiled Constable. "No scientific basis."

"Hmm, yes ... right." The doctor cleared his throat. "Anyway, apart from that, he's a literary critic - does a weekly column in one of the Sundays, which I have been known to read. Not what you'd call a man who's easily impressed - in fact, he specialises in hatchet jobs."

"So someone's done their own hatchet job on him, have they?"

"Not quite." And as Sergeant Copper re-emerged into the

Secret Garden to join them, "Come and take a look." The doctor held back the entrance flap of the tent and gestured the two detectives inside.

The interior of the tent was gloomy, with two squat flickering candles on stands making hardly any impression on the low light level. The air was still heavy with the smell of incense from joss sticks which had burned out on a side table, whose top was also scattered with packs of cards, what appeared to be small bone tokens, a carved wooden block, and a bundle of sticks decorated with Chinese symbols. Tucked alongside the table, and almost concealed by it, a suitcase.

The body of Horace Cope was sprawled forward across a small table covered with a black velvet cloth bearing a design of signs of the zodiac. He wore an exotic wide-sleeved robe in bright blue and gold, whose matching turban lay discarded on the ground to the side of the table. His face could not be seen - the back of his head was a very different matter. In a mass of blood and matted hair, through which Constable thought he could also see white splinters of bone, a large globe of some dark kind of glass nestled.

Inspector Constable had seen violent death in many forms, but even he had never been greeted with a spectacle quite like this.

"What the hell's that?" He gestured towards the dead man's head.

"That, I think you'll find, is Horace Cope's crystal ball. Looks to me like obsidian - that's a sort of volcanic glass, very expensive and very heavy."

"How heavy?"

"Oh, not so heavy that it couldn't be used by a man or a woman, if that's what you're getting at. Quite effective as a murder weapon though, by the look of it. Standard part of the fortune-teller's stock-in-trade, I believe. Gaze into the crystal, see what's in the future."

"Well, it doesn't look as if he saw that coming, did he, sir?" put in Sergeant Copper. "He's definitely got his ball in his brains, hasn't he?"

"Yes, thank you for the humorous take on the situation, Copper," said the inspector. "If we want jokes, we'll ask for them." Turning to the doctor, he enquired, "I take it there's not much doubt as to the cause of death?"

"None at all, in my opinion," agreed the doctor cheerfully, "but I'll let you know if it's any different once I've taken him away and had a good look at him."

"Time of death?"

"Oh, you don't need me for that. I gather he'd only just arrived at the Hall about half an hour before he was found just before One. Right, I must get on. Nothing else I can do here for now, so if you can get him sent round to my mortuary I'll get him on the slab and see if there's anything else I can get out of him." The doctor chuckled. "You know they always open up for me."

"Doctor," remarked Constable, "you are an extremely ghoulish man! You really do enjoy death, don't you?"

"It's a living," grinned the doctor, and with a cheery wave, he was gone.

"Right, Copper," said Constable briskly. "Let's get sorted. For a start, you can get on the phone, get Mr. Cope taken away, and find out where SOCO are. Somebody should have been here by now, unless they want us to do the whole job by ourselves." And as the sergeant reached into his pocket, "While you're at it, hold back that tent flap. This place smells like a tart's boudoir, and I can't see a damn thing in here."

While Dave Copper was murmuring into his mobile, Andy Constable slowly circled the dead man's body. Horace Cope's head was turned slightly to one side as it rested on the table, and as the inspector leaned forward to look more closely, he was met with a dull gleam from one still-open eye beneath an eyebrow seemingly raised in surprise. Plump almost lady-like hands, with a modest single gold signet ring on the left little finger, lay relaxed on the tabletop.

"Everybody's on their way, guv," said Copper as he re-entered the tent. "About ten minutes. So, what do you reckon?"

"It looks to me as if he was taken completely by surprise," said Constable. "Look at those hands. He's obviously made no attempt to defend himself. Plus, whoever did this must have been standing behind him, and it's not as if they could have sneaked up on him, because there's only the one entrance to the tent. So I reckon they knew each other. Right, let's see what else we've got." He turned his attention to the items lying

35

on the side table.

"Do you know anything about this clairvoyance business then, sir?" enquired Copper.

"Only enough to know that it could get you hanged for witchcraft a few hundred years ago. But all these bits and pieces are nothing special - you can get them in any of these new-age arty-crafty shops. Look here - you've got tarot cards ... Chinese fortune-telling sticks ... these little things are runes ... oh, now that's rather nice."

"What is it, sir?"

"That, sergeant, is a zodiac chart. Plots your future through the stars. Very Nostradamus. Very nicely-drawn constellations, loads of Latin notes all over it, but if I had to guess, I'd say it was probably French, sixteenth century."

"Valuable, sir?"

"Unfortunately not. Just a modern reproduction from the original woodcut."

Dave Copper was impressed. "Here, guv, you really do know a lot about this stuff, don't you?"

"The benefit of having had a half-decent education," smiled Constable. "Which is why I am a detective inspector, and you are but a humble sergeant. Right, get hold of that suitcase, and we'll see if there's anything helpful in there."

Copper knelt to open the suitcase. "Not a lot in here, sir. Little plastic box - it's got crayons in it, by the look of it. Why on earth would he want crayons? Anyway ... velvet bag ...." He passed it to the inspector, who emptied the contents on to the side table. The facets of the coloured stones gleamed in the candlelight.

"Bloody hell, sir! Are those jewels?"

"Don't get your hopes up, Copper. They're just crystals - semi-precious stones. I would tell you what they all are, but you're too easily impressed, and there's a limit to the amount of adulation I can take in one day. I think they use them for healing or adjusting your chakra or some such nonsense. Just another of Mr. Cope's tools of the trade."

"So not an attempted robbery that went wrong, then?"

"Not so far. What else is in there?"

"Just a jacket with ... a wallet in the inside pocket."

"Containing ...?"

Dave Copper opened the wallet and browsed through. "A hundred quid in twenties plus an odd fiver ... couple of bank cards ... store card for Harridges ... driving licence ... 'Crystal Cottage, Sloe Lane'."

"That's useful to know," remarked Constable. "We'll go along there and take a look round if we can't find much here. Is that it?"

"Hallo, hallo, what's all this then?"

"Copper, if you do that one more time, you are definitely back to traffic duty! What have we got?"

"A rather interesting newspaper cutting, sir," beamed the sergeant. "I think our Mr. Cope had a few naughty little secrets. Take a look at that." He handed the cutting to his colleague.

The small greyish piece of paper appeared to have been cut from the classified section of a newspaper. The column was headed 'Personal Services', and invited interested readers to telephone a main number followed by an access code in order to contact the various advertisers. Amongst the services on offer were Discreet Massage from a Lady at your Home or Hotel; A Personal Trainer offering to Work on your Body (Gareth - Press-ups a Speciality); and a French Lady who would provide Language Lessons in a Disciplined Atmosphere. One entry was circled in green ink. It read, "Escort and Photo Model. Full escort service for very demanding gentlemen. Souvenir photos also available. Call ' L'."

"How very interesting," commented Constable. "Now the question is, was Mr. Cope an existing customer or was he in the market for a bit of extra spice in his life? I wonder who 'L' is."

"They reckon some men develop odd tastes after they pass forty, sir," said Copper in an elaborately matter-of-fact voice. "Mid-life crisis, apparently."

"Traffic duty, sergeant?"

"Sorry, guv. Only kidding."

"Or ..." Inspector Constable paused. "Now here's a thought. Maybe Mr. Cope wasn't a customer at all. Maybe 'L' was somebody he knew. Maybe it wasn't his secret, but somebody else's."

"Well, we can't very well ask him, can we, sir? Perhaps there's something at his cottage."

A murmur of voices was heard, and the constable from the front gate put his head through the flap of the booth.

"Excuse me, inspector, but they've come to take the body away, and SOCO are here. Is it all right for them to come through?"

"Yes," replied Constable. "We're pretty much finished here for the time being." He stood aside as the overall-clad group of men entered the tent. "Oh, just one thing." He addressed the group's leader. "Let me know as soon as you can if there are any prints on that glass ball."

"Will do, sir."

"What next, guv?" Copper wanted to know. "Do we want to have a word with that lot in the house? Doesn't do to keep a Lady waiting, sir."

"I'm perfectly well aware of that, Copper. Just take a look through that door first - let's see what's on the other side of it."

Sergeant Copper rattled the handle of the door in the wall surrounding the garden. "Sorry, sir, it's locked. And no key. Shall I try and find one?"

"It'll keep for the moment. Come on, let's see who we've got indoors and what they can tell us."

"Hang about, sir. Have a look at this." Copper gestured to a pair of yellow rubber gloves lying almost invisible at the base of the tent wall. "Relevant, do you reckon?"

"Quite possibly, Copper, quite possibly. So what relevance might they have?"

Sergeant Copper thought for a moment. "Maybe the murderer wore them to handle the ball. In which case, we're not going to get any prints off it, are we? But ... we may get some DNA off the insides." He crouched to take a closer look. "No blood on them as far as I can see - just a couple of leaves stuck to them, but they could have come from these." He gestured to the adjacent flowerbeds.

"Sergeant, we may make a detective of you yet," smiled Constable. "Get SOCO to bag them, and we'll go and see what we can find out in the lions' den." He headed towards the house.

Chapter 4

A tense silence reigned in the drawing room of Dammett Hall as the detectives entered the room. At once, Sandra Lawdown surged towards Andy Constable.

"Inspector, thank goodness you're here. Now we can get this awful business sorted out."

"Good afternoon, your ladyship. We'll certainly do our best. This is my sergeant - Detective Sergeant Copper."

"Oh ... yes, of course." Lady Lawdown dismissed the very idea of the lower ranks with a nod and turned to the others in the room. "Everyone, this is Inspector Constable." The room murmured a greeting. "He's a marvel. I can't tell you the number of times I've had him in my court ..." She broke off with a laugh. "Giving evidence, of course. I wouldn't want anyone to get the wrong idea! Anyway, he always gets his man, or whatever it is you do when you're not a Mountie. That's why I asked for him specially. Your Chief Constable really is very sweet, you know."

Sergeant Copper, who had never heard the Chief referred to in quite such terms before, seemed to have difficulty in avoiding choking.

"I think we'd better make a start, your ladyship, if you don't mind," said Constable with a sideways glare at his colleague.

"Oh do, do. I have to tell you, I'm absolutely furious."

"Yes, it must be very upsetting to have a murder in your house. And I imagine Mr. Cope was a close friend ...?"

"What? Oh, I suppose so. No, I mean I'm furious because I've spent ages organising this year's fete, and now it's all been spoilt by that wretched little man getting himself killed!"

Inspector Constable cleared his throat. "Of course, that is one way of looking at it, madam ..."

Lady Lawdown began to pace the room. "Sorry, Inspector. I know I should be more sympathetic, but sympathy isn't going to pay for my roof repairs, is it? Or the poor vicar's church roof, of course," she added hastily. "We're sharing the proceeds, you see." She paused by the fireplace as a new thought seemed to strike her. "Mind you, it could be good, in a way."

"How would that be exactly, madam?" put in Sergeant Copper, who was beginning to feel a sense of disorientation.

"Don't you see, Sergeant? We could just postpone for a bit, and then all the publicity would bring the crowds flocking in. We might make even more money. Of course, I'd have to replace Horace."

"That certainly would be necessary, my lady," commented Constable in dry tones. "Given the late Mr. Cope's current … indisposition."

"Oh, yes. Poor Horace. Actually, he was very good at what he did. Not a charlatan at all. Not like some of these other media clairvoyants. Oh sorry, darling." Lady Lawdown glanced over her shoulder towards the seated figure of Seymour Cummings. "No offence. Tell me, Inspector, did you ever read Horace's column?"

"Actually no, your ladyship," confessed Constable. "In fact, before today, I have to admit I'd never even heard of Mr. Cope."

"Goodness! That is a surprise. It was amazing, some of the things he could tell you." And with a brisk switch of tone, "Well, I won't keep you, Inspector, because I suppose you must get on."

"If we may. Is there by any chance a room we can use?" He looked around the assembled company. "I shall need to speak to all of you, starting with the person who discovered Mr. Cope's body."

"That's the vicar," responded Lady Lawdown, "but he's upstairs at the moment. Poor man, he came tottering in, gasped out that he'd found Horace, and went out like a light. When he came round we poured a brandy down him and sent him upstairs to lie down. Laura will fetch him for you, won't you, darling. And I suppose you'd better use the library if you want to talk to people. There's nobody in there."

Dave Copper couldn't help himself. "No Body in the Library, eh? I bet that makes a nice change." Six pairs of eyes gazed at him blankly. From alongside him came a low growl from his superior officer. "Sorry."

After a moment's frozen pause, Lady Lawdown resumed

as if nothing had happened. "Laura darling, would you show the gentlemen the way. I'm going to have another drink, if you don't mind, Inspector. I'm absolutely frazzled." She turned back to the drinks table.

Laura Biding led the detectives back into the hall and closed the drawing room door behind them.

"Can we just check the layout of the house first, miss," enquired Sergeant Copper. "It may be important."

"Certainly, sergeant. What would you like to know?"

"What's through that door there?" Copper gestured to the door opposite the drawing room door.

"That's the dining room, but we hardly ever use it these days, unless Mother's having a big dinner party. We usually eat in the morning room - that's this door opposite the flower room corridor, and you know where that goes."

Dave Copper poked his head through the green baize door to refresh his memory. "And these doors in here?"

"That one on the right goes through to the kitchen, the one next door is just a loo, and the one on the left leads back into the dining room. Whoever designed this house was really quite clever," Laura remarked, as Copper rejoined her in the hall. "We actually get our food hot. This door here on the left doesn't actually lead to the kitchen - it's just a dummy to match the library door. And the library's in here."

She opened a door at the foot of the stairs and gestured her companions inside. The detectives entered a leather-furnished room with dark oak panelling and two book-lined walls. Heavy velvet curtains subdued the light from the windows, which gave on to the lawns and lake.

"This will do very nicely, miss," said Inspector Constable. "Thank you."

Laura Biding hesitated on the threshold of the room. "Inspector ..."

"Yes, miss?"

"You'll have to forgive my mother - she's got a funny way of looking at things sometimes. I'd hate you to get the wrong impression."

"Not at all, Miss Biding. It is 'Miss', is it? I mean, you being her ladyship's daughter. Or is it 'The Honourable'? We wouldn't want to cause offence by getting it wrong."

Laura smiled. "No, Inspector, just plain Laura Biding. My dad was Mother's first husband, so I don't get a title. But I don't think anyone worries about things like that these days, do they? So, would you like me to go up and fetch Mr. Pugh?"

"I think we can leave the vicar for a little later, miss. If he was as shocked as your mother said, it sounds as if a bit of a rest might not go amiss. But if we can just have a word with you first..."

"Would you like me to take notes, sir?" Copper seemed keen to return to the investigation.

"Thank you for the reminder, sergeant," replied the inspector with a shade of annoyance. "Please take a seat, Miss Biding. Although it seems a little odd to invite you to sit down in your own house, but I'm afraid we do have to ask you some questions about Mr. Cope's murder."

"Poor Uncle Horace! Isn't it awful!"

"Uncle Horace? You mean he was ..."

"Oh no," responded Laura hastily. "Don't misunderstand me. I called him Uncle, but he wasn't actually a relative - he was one of those old friends of the family. He's been around forever, and he was always buying me presents and taking me out to the theatre or for meals and so on. I expect it was because I was an only child. Perhaps he thought I was lonely."

"So, very close then?"

"I think he even introduced my mother to my stepfather. Sorry, that's Lord Lawdown, of course. It's a bit complicated, isn't it?" She looked up wide-eyed at Andy Constable.

"I think we get the general gist, miss," the inspector reassured her. "And Lord Lawdown himself died a little while ago, I believe."

"Yes," assented Laura. "So my mother's a widow now. Twice over, actually."

"So your real father ...?"

"Oh, he died when I was a tiny child. I hardly remember him at all. It wasn't the sort of thing that got talked about when I was growing up."

"No, of course, miss. I quite understand." Inspector Constable thought for a moment. "Can you tell me who was in the house at the time of the murder."

Laura reflected. "There was Mother and me, and we had

42

a few people in for drinks before the start of the fete. There's Seymour, who's staying with us ... Mother's friend Helen from the village ... Robin, that's another friend ... Horace's cousin Albert ... and of course Mr. Pugh. That's the vicar - he was supposed to open the fete at one o'clock. Oh, I almost forgot - Amelia Cook was in the kitchen because Mother asked her to do the catering. Amelia runs the village tearooms, you see. Good Lord - I hope she's not still in there making sandwiches!"

"Don't worry, miss, we'll check on that. So you're sure that nobody else was in the house at the time of the crime? No servants?"

"No, we don't have any live-in staff. There's Mrs. Richards who comes up from the village in the mornings to do the cleaning, but she's always gone long before mid-day, which is when Uncle Horace arrived."

"Could anyone else have gained access to the house without you knowing? After all, you did have a large number of people in the grounds."

"I can't see how. The front door was open, but I'm sure nobody could have got past the drawing room without being seen. We always keep the house quite secure these days. We had a burglary a few months ago - nothing too serious, mostly just a few pieces of silver, but there's not really all that much in the way of valuables left to steal these days. Anyway, after that, we always make sure that the doors are locked."

"What doors are there, miss?" asked Sergeant Copper. "I am going to have to check."

"Not that many, actually. There is a door to the kitchen from the stable yard, but that's one of the ones we keep locked, and Amelia was in there anyway. The french windows in this room and the drawing room are always bolted, and so are the ones out on to the west terrace from the dining room. The door from the flower room is usually open, but the terrace only leads to the Secret Garden anyway, and the gate in there is always locked."

"We know that, miss," replied Copper. "We tried it. Can you let us have a key, please."

"Certainly, sergeant. There's one hanging on a hook in the flower room. I used it yesterday. Would you like me to fetch it for you?"

"If you wouldn't mind, Miss Biding," said Inspector Constable. "I think that's all for the moment. If you could just pop the key in to us, and then ask the other lady if she could come through."

Laura Biding left the library, and reappeared in only a matter of seconds. "I'm sorry, inspector. That key ... it's gone."

*

Helen Highwater knocked at the library door.

"Please come in, madam. Have a seat." Dave Copper indicated a chair in front of the desk, behind which Inspector Constable had taken position. The sergeant seated himself unobtrusively near the fireplace.

"I'm afraid I have to ask you some questions about today's events, madam. We'll try not to keep you too long."

"Oh, I quite understand, inspector. You have your duty to do. And Sandra says you're very good, so I'm sure you'll have everything sorted out in a tick. Sandra's such a good judge of character."

"Sandra?"

"Oh, I'm so sorry, inspector. I meant Lady Lawdown, of course. I forgot that you don't know her as well as I do. Yes, we've known each other for years. Ever since she came to live here, which of course is ages ago now. And her husband was a dear, dear friend. Now he was a lovely man. Such a shame he died. I was very upset. But Sandra just picked herself up and got on with everything. Said she had to keep the Lawdown flag flying over the Hall, so she carried on with all the traditions, and she's so devoted to public service, and of course things like the fete are so important in a village like this, don't you agree? So that's why we were all here today, because Sandra always has a little party for a few of her friends just before the fete starts, and of course she asked me, and I think I was the first to arrive. So ..." She took a deep breath. "How can I help you?"

The inspector blinked. "I think we'd better start with your name, please."

"Sorry, inspector. I've got used to everybody knowing who I am. It's living in a village, I suppose. I'm Helen Highwater." Inspector Constable's face registered no recognition. "The author ..."

"Forgive me, Mrs. Highwater ..."

44

"Miss."

"I beg your pardon ... Miss Highwater." The inspector was apologetic. "I'm afraid I'm not terribly well up on authors."

"Oh, but I'm sure you must have heard of my books about my schoolgirl magician, Carrie Otter. But of course, that's under my pen name of Jake A. Rawlings."

"You're Jake A. Rawlings?" interrupted Copper, astonished. "You wrote the Carrie Otter books? That's amazing. Those books are great!"

"Do you have children then, sergeant?" enquired Helen.

Dave Copper blushed. "Actually, no, Miss Highwater. I mean, I read them myself." And in response to Inspector Constable's quizzical look, "I happen to think they're very exciting. I reckon I must be one of your biggest fans."

"That's very kind of you to say so, sergeant. I have to confess, sometimes I can't believe how successful they've become myself. I've had so many awards for my latest book - 'Carrie Otter and the ...'"

"... Half-Boiled Pants'!" joined in the sergeant in chorus. "Oh, that one was brilliant. I loved the bit where Carrie, Don, and Evadne drink the Multimix Medicine and then ..."

"Of course we're very familiar with your works, Miss Highwater," broke in Inspector Constable, determined to regain control of an interview which seemed in danger of wandering from the point, "but I'm afraid we don't really have time to discuss them now. We have the rather more pressing matter of Mr. Cope's death to investigate."

"Ah, yes, Horace." A note of reserve entered Helen's voice. "Of course, you can't please everyone all the time, and I'm afraid Horace was not quite as kind about my last book as you, sergeant. In fact, I thought that he could have been more polite in his review column, but of course we authors have to put up with a little criticism from time to time. But I've never been one to hold a grudge." She smiled brightly. "So, yes ... Horace. I suppose you want to ask me where I saw him and when, and all those other searching questions. I've read all those detective books, you know. Of course, I've never actually written one, because I don't know that I have the sort of mind to work out all those intricate things about alibis and motives and forensics and so on. It's so much easier with Carrie, you see. If she gets

45

into a tight spot, I just get her to do a bit of magic, and it seems to solve everything. I expect you wish you could do that sometimes, inspector. It would make your job so much easier, wouldn't it, as well as ..."

"So what can you tell us about Mr. Cope's movements today?" Inspector Constable forced his way into Helen's increasingly rambling flow.

"Well ... hardly anything, really." The inspector barely stopped himself sighing. "As I say, I was here first, and then Laura came in, and the poor dear was absolutely worn out because she'd been rushing about all morning - it's always like that on the day of the fete, and really it's a miracle that she stays as calm as she does, and I know for a fact that I could never do half as good a job with all the organisation ..." She tailed off. "Now, where was I?"

"You had just arrived, madam." Sergeant Copper's calm voice was a contrast to Helen's breathless twittering. "And Miss Biding had come in ..."

"That's right. It's so important to be clear, isn't it? Oh yes, and then Mr. Pugh appeared, and he was quite puffed out because he'd walked all the way up from the village, and the walk up from the front gates is a lot steeper than it seems when you're driving, and if only I'd noticed him I could have given him a lift in my little car. Ah ... yes!"

"Yes, Miss Highwater?" enquired Constable.

"Yes!" Helen was triumphant. "That was when Horace arrived! Just after the vicar. And he had Albert with him. But he didn't stay long, because he said he had to get his things set up, and he wanted Albert to do his make-up for him, but Laura persuaded Albert to stay for a drink, so off Horace went, and so that was that." She looked at Constable expectantly. "Will that do, inspector?"

There was one thing puzzling the inspector. "Make-up?"

"Oh, something about eyebrows," explained Helen airily. "I didn't really pay attention. All to do with his 'character', apparently. I don't understand all this showmanship. But I suppose people have their own ways of looking at things."

"I don't think we need to keep you any longer, Miss Highwater," said Inspector Constable. "But we may need to speak to you again later, so please don't leave the premises."

"Don't worry, inspector," replied Helen with dignity. "I don't intend to run away. I shall be staying to support Sandra - this can't be very nice for her. I'm a great believer in duty." She turned to Dave Copper. "Goodbye, sergeant. Thank you so much for all those kind things you said about my books. You must look out for the new book when it comes out next month - it's called 'Carrie Otter and the Deadly Pillows'. In fact, if you like, I'll sign a copy for you."

"That'd be wonderful."

"Well, it's the last chance you'll get. It is the last in the series, and I think it's the best, but of course, we'll have to wait to see what the public thinks. And there's a big secret ending, but I'm not going to spoil the surprise for you." And with a twinkle, she was gone.

*

"I appear to be next in line for the inquisition, inspector." Seymour Cummings entered the library with an air of calm self-assurance. "I take it this is the interrogation chair. What would you like to know?"

"I think your name would be most helpful to begin with, if you don't mind, please, sir." Andy Constable's affable smile and warm tone did not deceive Dave Copper, who winced internally. He knew that his superior officer was always inclined to dislike and distrust over-confidence in a murder suspect.

"My name is Seymour Cummings." He turned to Dave Copper. "Do you need me to spell that for you, sergeant?"

"I don't think that'll be necessary, sir. I have heard of you." He smiled in his turn. "The ... er ... gentleman is a newspaper clairvoyant, sir," he explained to his superior.

"Another? Well ..." Constable let the sentence hang in the air. "And how did you come to be here today, Mr. Cummings?"

"I happened to be staying with Sandra Lawdown for a few days. I do that quite often. We've known each other for years. Oh, nothing of that kind," he explained hastily. "We're just good friends, if you'll pardon the cliché."

"And you were also acquainted with the late Mr. Cope, I assume?"

"Yes, inspector. In fact, you're absolutely right to put me in the frame. I suppose you could say that Horace Cope and I

47

were deadly enemies."

"Really, sir? In what way?" Andy Constable leaned forward intently.

"Now don't get me wrong, inspector. That was just a joke. On reflection, not a particularly funny one. But Horace had his column in the Evening Sin, and I have mine in the Daily Stir, and you know what newspapers are like. They're always trying to get one over on their competitors - it's all to do with circulation and advertising revenue and all the sordid financial side of things. The trouble is, so often the contributors get caught up in it and it all turns very nasty. I'm sure you've heard of spoiler headlines and people stealing exclusives and all sorts of dirty tricks. Nothing of that sort between Horace and me, of course. It was a friendly rivalry, really. Professional."

"So, Mr. Cummings, what did you think of Mr. Cope?" asked Constable. "Professionally speaking, of course."

"To be honest, inspector, I didn't really think he was that good, but I suppose you'd expect me to say that. Sometimes he got things right by chance and pinched all the headlines, which of course drove me and all my colleagues in the business mad, but I don't think you'll find a motive for murder there."

"How do you mean, sir?"

"Don't you remember that business with the jewellery, inspector? It was in London." Seymour leaned back in his chair and seemed prepared to enjoy himself. "There was a French Countess of ... oh, somewhere-or-other staying at the Dorchester House Hotel, and she had an emerald necklace stolen, which used to belong to the Empress Josephine, and goodness knows what else besides. And, if you'll forgive another cliché, the police were baffled. Interviewed everyone from the manager to all the guests to the hotel cat, and ended up with not the faintest idea of who was responsible. Of course, by this time, the lady was having screaming fits, so in desperation the Count called in Horace. And damn me, but the blighter told the police where to find the jewels. I have no idea how he did it, but of course it was all over the papers, mine included, which I was not terribly pleased about, as you can imagine. Still no reason for doing him in, though. And as for his book critic's column - well, that was complete rubbish. Just a load of bile. Not very good at all."

"So you're telling us that you had no reason to do Mr. Cope harm," enquired the inspector.

"None in the world, I'm afraid," replied Seymour. "And in fact, as for today, I didn't even see the man. I was out for a walk when he arrived, and by the time I came back, I gather he'd already gone out to his tent to set up his paraphernalia. After which I was in the house until the vicar reappeared looking like death warmed up, and broke the ghastly news to us all. So that's about it."

"In which case, I'll let you go for the moment, sir, but we may need to ask you some further questions later." And as Seymour rose and was about to leave the room, "Oh, just one thing, sir. Somebody mentioned something about a television programme ...?"

There was a slight pause before Seymour turned back. "Oh ... you know about that, do you? Yes, of course, 'Seeing Stars'. Yes, Horace and I were both in line to present it. Something of a plum job. Well, I think I can predict that Horace won't be getting that, will he?"

*

The tap at the library door was so diffident as to be almost inaudible.

"Come in," called Inspector Constable. No reaction. "Come in!" Still nothing. "It's one of those days, isn't it," he added in exasperation. "Copper, find out who that is, and get them in here before I die of old age."

Sergeant Copper admitted Albert Ross into the library and gestured him to the chair facing Inspector Constable at the desk. Albert seemed twitchy, and his eyes darted round the room before finally settling on the inspector. He licked his lips.

"I'm sorry to have kept you waiting, sir." Andy Constable spoke smoothly and without haste. It was obviously going to be necessary to keep things calm if the witness was to provide anything useful. "I'm afraid these things always take longer than they should. If you could tell us who you are, please, just so my sergeant can make a few notes."

"My name is Albert Ross, er ... inspector, isn't it? I'm Horace's cousin."

"Do forgive me, Mr. Ross. I had no idea. My condolences, sir. Were you and your cousin particularly close?"

"Oh indeed yes, inspector. Horace has been an absolute rock. He's my only relative, you see."

"Indeed, sir?"

"Yes, we came from a very small family. Our mothers were sisters, my father was an only child and so was Horace's, and neither he nor I had any brothers and sisters."

"And no family of your own?"

"No, inspector. I've never married, and of course, Horace ... well, er, no." He tailed off lamely.

"Thank you for that, sir." Inspector Constable's manner became brisker. "So, Mr. Ross, are you a local? Do you live in Dammett Worthy?"

"Well, yes and no." Albert smiled weakly. "I apologise, inspector, I'm not making myself very clear. It's not very easy to think straight. I'm not a local, no, because I come from London, which is where I used to live. But I'm living at Horace's cottage at present. I've been staying with Horace for - oh, ages now."

"Yes, sir?" Constable raised his eyebrows and waited.

Albert became flustered once again. "It's actually rather embarrassing. I had some bad luck with money a little while back - well, you know how things are, it's been the same for so many people. But I had some investments which didn't turn out too well, and then I lost my little flat in London, so Horace very kindly said I could stay with him until I got back on my feet. I mean, it's not as if there was anyone else I could turn to - he and I were the only members of the family left, so we only had each other. And now I suppose it's just me. Oh dear ..." He tailed off again, blinking, and dropped his head into his hands.

Andy Constable and Dave Copper exchanged glances, and the inspector nodded slightly. He leaned back in his chair, while Dave Copper moved to a low chair alongside Albert.

"Sorry to have to press you, sir, but I need you to tell me about Mr. Cope's movements today."

Albert sniffed, seemed to pull himself together, and sat upright.

"That's quite all right, sergeant," he said. "I know you have to ask. Just let me think a moment ..." Albert frowned in concentration. "It started off as quite an ordinary morning, really. You know, breakfast and so on, but I don't suppose you want to know about that. The post came, but I don't think there was anything in it except bills. Horace does most of his correspondence by email these days - I don't understand all that computer stuff. And then Horace spent some time getting his things together for this afternoon - his cards and crystal ball and all that. After that, he popped round to the flower shop, while I was busy doing the cleaning, because I like to keep the cottage nice for him. I feel it's the least I can do. Then Horace gave me everything to pack into a case to bring up here, and then I made us a cup of tea, and then we set out. I suppose that must have been about twenty to twelve. Is that what you wanted to know?"

"Did you drive?"

"Oh no, sergeant. I don't have a car, and Horace always likes to go for a walk every morning, so we walked. I carried the case." He sighed at the memory.

"And you reached here at what time?"

"I'm sure it was about five past twelve, because we were a little later than we meant to be, and Horace got rather annoyed with me. He wanted me to walk faster, you see, but with the case ..."

"And after you arrived at the Hall?"

"We went in," explained Albert pedantically. He seemed to have got into his stride. "Lady Lawdown gave us a drink, and then Horace wanted to carry on because we were late, so he went off on his own to start getting ready, and then I told her ladyship I really couldn't stay, because Horace wanted me to help him prepare and get him dressed and do his make-up. And then later on I was back with everyone else when the vicar came in and told us he'd found Horace. And I was so shocked, and I felt I ought to go to him, but after what Mr. Pugh told us, I just couldn't ...." He gulped and hid his face again.

Andy Constable took over again. "Please don't upset yourself, Mr. Ross. We have seen Mr. Cope, and it's probably for the best that you didn't go out there. I think we'll leave it there for the moment. It's been very helpful to understand some of the background."

"Horace has been so good to me," sniffed Albert, wiping his eyes, "and I haven't had to pay for a thing. He was a very generous man, you know, despite what some people may tell you about him. It's not easy to find a job when you get to my

51

age, but Horace said he was determined to sort something out. I really don't know what I shall do. I expect I shall stay on at the cottage for the moment, of course, but goodness knows after that."

"Ah, that reminds me, Mr. Ross," said Constable. "If you wouldn't mind, we may want to take a look round the cottage. You never know ..." He left the conclusion to Albert's imagination. "Do you happen to have a key with you? That's if you've no objection, of course."

"Um ... no, I don't mind at all, inspector. Do look round if you want. Do you want me to come with you? I'll need to disarm the burglar alarm." He fished in a pocket for a key.

"That won't be necessary, sir," replied Constable, who very much did not want Albert's assistance. Life was always easier if the owner of a property wasn't around during a search. "If you don't mind giving us the code, we'll deal with all that."

As Albert left the library, the two policemen exchanged looks.

"Make-up again, sir. That must be what those crayon things were in the case."

"Exactly, Copper. In the case. But on Mr. Cope, not a sausage. So what do you make of that?"

*

"Good afternoon, Detective Inspector." Robin Allday advanced confidently, his hand held out to shake Andy Constable's. "We have met, but I don't know if you'll remember me. Robin Allday."

"Of course I remember you, Mr. Allday," smiled the inspector. "Do please have a seat. I can remember a couple of people you've managed to get off, who we would rather have seen end up with a criminal record. And I think I've seen you around the station a few times. I wasn't aware that you were a local."

"Yes, I'm based in Dammett Worthy. Hall, Knight and Allday, in the High Street. It sounds far grander than it is, I'm afraid. Actually it's just a one-man band - well, me and my secretary. Just an ordinary country practice, really - I hardly ever get involved with court proceedings, which is why I thought I might not ring a bell with you."

"We have famously long memories for names and faces,

Mr. Allday. Not of course a problem for anyone who stays on the right side of the law." The inspector laughed. "So which side of the law are you on, Mr. Allday?"

"What ... oh, I see what you mean," said Robin. "A bit slow on the uptake there, I'm afraid. It's difficult to be at your sharpest when there's murder going on. The worst we usually get around here is the odd poacher getting in the way of a few shotgun pellets." He took a breath. "Sorry, inspector - I'm rambling. You asked about my practice. I suppose I do pretty much all the legal work around these parts - you know, wills, conveyancing, financial trusts, that sort of stuff. We do like to keep things local - it's a very close-knit community here in Dammett Worthy."

"And did that community include Mr. Cope?" enquired Constable.

"Yes," replied Robin, "I was Horace's solicitor. As a matter of fact, I was engaged in some work for him at the moment, but of course I can't really talk about that - rules about client confidentiality and all that, which I'm sure you know all about."

"So being Mr. Cope's solicitor, presumably you may have made a will for him," asked Constable. "Or are you not allowed to tell me that either?"

"Oh, I can tell you that all right," said Robin. "Yes, there is a will, but I can't tell you what's in it. Not yet, at any rate. I'm afraid you'll need a court order to see it if you want to do so in a hurry. Why, do you think you will?"

"I really can't tell at this stage, Mr. Allday. It may be relevant, it may not. Of course, we do have a magistrate handy on the premises - I don't suppose Lady Lawdown's authority would be sufficient, would it."

Robin took in the smile on Inspector Constable's face. "Now you're just teasing, inspector. You know that isn't the way things work. I don't make the rules, you know - I just have to follow them." The inspector continued to gaze at him. "Look, if it helps you, you may not know that Albert Ross is Horace's only living relative."

"Yes, we were aware of that, Mr. Allday."

"Well then, inspector, you might like to draw your own conclusions from that. That's all I can say."

"Thank you, sir. That's very helpful. Now, about this afternoon ..."

"I don't know that I can be at all helpful on that score. I was hardly here at all. I should have been here at twelve o'clock because Lady Lawdown had invited a few of us for drinks before the fete. But I went into the office this morning, because sometimes Saturday morning is the only chance I get to catch up with things. I only meant to stay for half an hour, but you know what it's like, inspector. Sometimes you just get bogged down in paperwork."

"Yes, sir, I know that only too well," groaned Constable ruefully.

"So there I was, ploughing through these documents, and they're never as simple as you hope they're going to be. Of course, I completely lost track of time. The next thing I knew, Laura's on the phone to ask me where I am, so I came straight on up. But by the time I got here, Horace had already gone out to his tent, so I didn't see him, and it was only a couple of minutes after that when we all heard the shocking news from Mr. Pugh. Actually, I was the one who called the police while they were taking the vicar upstairs. And then Lady Lawdown got on to your Chief Constable because I think she knows him quite well. I believe she asked for you in person."

"So I understand, sir," said Andy Constable drily.

"That's about all I can tell you. So ... well, now you know as much as I do."

"People are always saying that to me, Mr. Allday," said the inspector. "And sometimes it's actually true, sir. But I think we'll settle for that for now. We have some other matters to look into, so I may want your help again later."

"You only have to ask, Mr. Constable. You know where to find me."

"Indeed I do, Mr. Allday." Andy Constable's tone was carefully neutral.

Robin's look seemed to be trying to gauge whether a deeper meaning lay behind the inspector's words. With a shaky smile, he left the room.

"So what do you make of our Mr. Allday, then, sergeant?" asked Inspector Constable.

"I reckon he's worried about something, sir. Couldn't say

what, though. Shall I get him back in?"

"No, I think we'll let him stew for a while. I may be wrong, but I'm not sensing the right sort of guilt. If it's anything relevant, I dare say it will trickle out later. At the moment, I'm more concerned with taking a look around Mr. Cope's cottage. Like the book says, the more you know about the victim ..."

"I take it I'm driving again then, sir?"

Chapter 5

The Dammett Worthy constable had now taken up position at the front door of the Hall, looking as if he expected to repel hordes of ghoulish sight-seers and was rather embarrassed at the fact. He stood aside as Andy Constable emerged. The inspector allowed himself a quiet smile at the young man's mixture of enthusiasm and self-consciousness.

"Right then, Cerberus ..."

"No, sir. Collins, sir. P.C. Collins, sir."

Inspector Constable sighed. "Of course. All right, Collins, I'm leaving you in charge of the scene while I go off and look at the dead man's cottage. I don't want any of the people in the house wandering off while I'm away."

"Right, sir. Thank you, sir. Leave it to me, sir." He drew himself up and snapped a salute.

Andy Constable kept a straight face. "So let's have a bit of your local knowledge. How do I get to Sloe Lane?"

*

The drive to the village took only a few minutes, and the detectives parked the car on the green in front of the church. The rambling building in the local mellow grey stone nestled in a picturesque churchyard filled with a random muddle of tilting headstones, family tombs with moss-filled inscriptions, and Victorian monuments surrounded by fearsome wrought-iron railings, all overhung by huge horse-chestnut trees in full leaf and a monumental yew, its limbs propped on timber supports, close to the lych-gate.

"Nice church, sir," commented Dave Copper appreciatively.

"A bit of everything," replied Andy Constable. "Norman originally, I should think, and they've added a bit every century or so. But that reminds me - we must have a talk with the vicar when we get back to the Hall."

"That's if he's got over his fit of the vapours," grinned Copper.

"Right, then - Mr. Cope's cottage. Let's see what we can find out about our dead man."

56

Crystal Cottage stood back a little from Sloe Lane, fronted by a classic country cottage garden filled with a profusion of old-fashioned flowers. The long low building featured every picture postcard cliché, from tiny windows with leaded lights, courses of flint set into the traditional local stone of the front wall, and dormer windows which peeped through an immaculately groomed thatch adorned with a straw pheasant at the apex. Polished brass gleamed on the sturdy oak front door. Twisted terracotta chimney-pots spoke of a history reaching back to Queen Elizabeth I. A black cat dozed in a sunlit spot on a rockery, and opened one lazy eye as Constable and Copper advanced up the path.

"Looks as if Mr. Cope did quite well for himself," remarked Copper. "I bet this place is worth a few quid. You couldn't really get much better, could you?"

"Hmm." Andy Constable was more reserved. "Very pretty. He's even got roses round the door. The only trouble is, it's a bit too perfect for my liking. I never trust perfection."

The detectives let themselves into a dark hall of beams and panelling, whose walls were hung with an unexpected mixture of historic maps of the county and carved wooden African tribal masks. At the rear of the hall could be seen a surprisingly modern kitchen gleaming with stainless steel and black tile, while ahead an oak staircase led upstairs. To the right lay a small parlour, obviously used as an office with desktop computer and box files, while a large sitting-room could be seen through the half-opened door to the left. A low buzz sounded from behind the front door, where the red eye of a burglar alarm winked at the officers. Inspector Constable punched in the number Albert had given him. The red eye gazed at him steadily.

"Are we looking for anything in particular, sir?" asked Copper.

"Frankly, sergeant, I have absolutely no idea," replied Constable. "But from what I've seen and heard so far, Mr. Cope doesn't seem to have been your ordinary chap who gets bashed on the head for an ordinary domestic reason. Our Mr. Cope was a bit exotic. So let's just have a poke about and see if we can find out just how exotic he was. We might as well start at the top." He led the way upstairs.

The landing at the head of the stairs offered the choice of three doors. Constable opened the one on the right, revealing a sparse bedroom containing a single bed with an oaken bedside cabinet, a small matching wardrobe, a chest of drawers, and little else. A bedside lamp. A photograph of an elderly lady in a silver frame. A sponge-bag on a bentwood chair. An overall air of obsessive neatness.

"Spare room, sir," said Copper over his superior's shoulder. "Mr. Ross's, I suppose."

"Not a lot of personality, is there?"

"The room or Mr. Ross, sir?"

"You work it out, sergeant. Have a browse through the cupboards on the off-chance, though, and let me know if there's anything worth a second look." And as Sergeant Copper began to open the drawers of the chest, "And if there's anything other than beige, call the Yard."

"Will do, sir."

The bathroom next door was a shock. Far larger than the spare bedroom, it was fitted from floor to ceiling in marble, with a free-standing Victorian bath on ball-and-claw feet standing almost belligerently in the centre of the floor. Ornate mirrors in gold rococo frames hung on two walls, reflecting the gold taps and fittings of an extravagant dolphin design. Glass jars held coloured balls of cotton wool. Perfumed soaps from a Piccadilly store lay in porcelain scallop-shells. Enormous peach towels monogrammed 'HC' were draped voluptuously across a brocade armchair. "Very footballer's wife," thought Constable with a shudder of distaste. A brief glance into the bathroom cabinet revealed nothing more interesting than headache pills, mouthwash, and a tube of ointment whose use the inspector preferred not to investigate too closely. He moved on to the third door.

After the bathroom, Horace Cope's bedroom came as no great surprise. The room was dominated by a huge carved half-tester bed draped with opulent curtains in purple and gold, kept barely under control with chubby gold tassels. A cabinet of brass-inlaid rosewood bearing several bottles of extremely expensive after-shave seemed to serve as a dressing-table. A spindly-legged regency sofa, upholstered to match the bed hangings, simpered beneath the window. On one wall hung a mirror in a surround of sixteenth-century stump-work, next to a group of Georgian miniatures. On another, a tapestry of a classical hunting scene. Underfoot, polished floorboards were scattered with a selection of silk rugs which the inspector instinctively felt would have cost him several months' salary. Behind the door, and occupying the entire wall, a gigantic three-doored Victorian wardrobe held an impressive selection of suits, shirts, and hand-made shoes from well-known London makers. Inspector Constable raised his eyes to the ceiling. It was painted black, with the signs of the zodiac picked out in gold. The design struck a chord in the inspector's memory, which he struggled for a moment to identify. Then he realised where he had seen it before. In the fortune-teller's booth - the pattern of the tablecloth across which Horace Cope's body had been slumped.

Briskly and professionally, Andy Constable searched through cupboards and wardrobes, with an irritating lack of success. Nothing, other than a flamboyant taste in ties which toned well with the bedroom which housed them, met his eye. He turned his attention to the bed, where a book bound in maroon leather lay on the pillow. "Let's take a look at Mr. Cope's bedtime reading," said Constable half-aloud, and found himself leafing through the pages of what appeared to be a nineteenth-century French novel. The inspector's French did not do his seven years of study to A-level a great deal of credit, but it was good enough to grasp the main gist, and to tell him that the activities of the book's heroine would not have been accepted in the best society.

Dave Copper came into the bedroom and stopped short. "Bloody hell, sir, this is a bit of a contrast, isn't it?"

"You might very well say that, sergeant."

"Anything, sir?"

"Nothing I can put my finger on. Other than the fact that I don't reckon Mr. Cope was the sort of chap I'd have enjoyed having a pint with. Not that that's any reason for the man to get himself murdered. How about you?"

"Well, sir ..."

"Copper, you're looking smug. You really should be careful about doing that. It does not endear you to your superiors."

"No, sir. Sorry, sir."

"Come on, then, what have you got?"

Sergeant Copper led the way into the small bedroom and gestured to the bottom drawer of the chest. "Just this, sir. Mr. Ross's life savings, do you reckon?"

At the back of the drawer, and half-concealed behind several pairs of meticulously-folded socks, nestled a bundle of banknotes in a rubber band.

"Why is it always the sock drawer?" sighed Constable. "Has nobody got any originality any more?"

"Well, at least it saves us checking under the floorboards, sir," remarked Copper.

"Touched them?"

"No, sir. Didn't want to muck them about. But it looks as if they're all twenties, so I reckon there must be a good thousand quid there."

"More, I should think. Stick them in a bag, sergeant. We'll get them checked, although there are probably more prints on them than you can shake a stick at. And there may be nothing to it anyway. It's not a crime to stash a bundle of notes under your socks."

"Not unless you're not supposed to have them, sir. I thought Mr. Ross was meant to be on his uppers, from what he said to you. So who do you think he was hiding them from?"

"We shall have to ask him, shan't we?" replied Constable. "Right, you can do the kitchen, then you can get a bag from the car for those, while I take a look in Mr. Cope's living-room."

The sitting-room of the cottage was dominated by a large brick inglenook fireplace taking up one entire end of the room, whose ceiling and walls featured an excess of heavy dark oak beams. On one section of the wall, a glass panel protected an area of painted plaster showing a hunting scene which the inspector was confident dated from the cottage's early years. Around the rest of the room, the mixture of furnishings dated from every period of the building's history. A gilt pier table was surmounted by a looking-glass with a surround of palm leaves. A carved cabinet on legs, in the form of a classical temple, had its doors ajar to allow a glimpse of the intricate inlays of coloured marbles decorating the doors and drawers of the interior. Silver candlesticks and dishes gleamed on a table at the back of a monumental tasselled sofa in carved velvet. A glass-topped display cabinet, its sides inlaid with delicate marquetry of sphinxes and lotuses, harboured a sparse scatter of exquisite objects nestling on a bed of artfully-crumpled blue silk - a tiny jewelled prayer-book, a collection of 18th century miniatures, intricately-carved Japanese ivory netsukes, a pair of Jacobean embroidered leather gloves, a silver snuff-box, a Venetian glass bottle. French windows led to a paved courtyard garden in which could be glimpsed a cast-iron table and chairs.

"Well, Copper, what do you make of this lot?" asked Constable as his colleague reappeared at the foot of the stairs carrying the plastic bag of banknotes.

"It is my considered opinion, sir," replied Copper, "speaking as a trained detective who has worked under the best, that our Mr. Cope was not short of a bob or two. I assume it's all genuine, sir? You'd know that better than me."

"Very genuine as far as I can see, and worth a great deal of money. Some of the stuff in this cabinet is very valuable indeed. Mr. Cope obviously had the cash to indulge himself."

Dave Copper peered more closely at the cabinet's contents. "We're obviously in the wrong job, sir," he remarked. "Who knew the fortune-telling business paid so well?" A thought struck him. "Just one thing, sir ..."

"And what's that?"

"It's just that ... well, it's not exactly crammed full, is it, sir? I mean, compared with the rest of the house. You've got his bedroom and his bathroom, and you can't move for bits and pieces and knick-knacks. And then you come in here, and the room's full of stuff again, and yet here you've got this little cabinet with all these little things in it, which I'm guessing were his pride and joy, and ... well, there's a bit too much fresh air in it, to my way of thinking."

Inspector Constable bent forward over the cabinet. "Copper, there are times when I'm quite proud of you. That is a very intelligent piece of observation. And in fact ... yes, if you take a closer look, you can see the marks where there have been other things resting on the material."

"Of course, he might just have gone off stuff and sold it, sir," suggested Copper.

"Possible. But I get the feeling that Mr. Cope was more of

a collector than a disposer, somehow." Inspector Constable prowled the room in thought. "You've got me thinking, sergeant. Look at these gaps on the wall. There ought to be pictures there. You've still got the hooks, and if you look very carefully from the side you can see a sort of shadow outline of the frame that used to be there. So that doesn't seem to fit in, does it?"

"Sir, take a look here." Dave Copper gestured to the french windows. Around the catch, there were signs that a recent repair had taken place. Under the dark stain, a new piece of wood had been set into the original oak, and a new brass lock had been fitted. "Mr. Cope seems to have had uninvited callers."

"If he has, then that burglar alarm isn't up to much, is it? Right, anything I should know about in the kitchen?"

"Not a thing, sir. Shiny and expensive, and nothing much in the fridge except a rather nice looking bottle of champagne and a pint of milk. I get the feeling our dead man didn't cook much at home."

"Then we'd better take a look at Mr. Cope's office," said Constable. "With a bit of luck, we've saved the best for last."

In contrast with the rest of the house, the study was spartan and business-like. Bookshelves lined one wall, bearing a variety of works which would have done credit to the library of a small country town. One section was entirely devoted to books on the occult, spiritualism, clairvoyance, and astrology. Behind glazed doors lay a selection of packs of tarot cards, coloured crystals, figurines of oriental deities, and incense burners. A shelf of box files held several years' worth of back copies of psychic magazines and newspapers, prominently featuring 'Future News' and the Conjurers' Association 'Witch' magazine, together with what was clearly an archive of cuttings of Horace Cope's columns and articles. A fairly-obviously-hinged modern oil painting of a robed druid at Stonehenge revealed a small wall-safe. And on a chrome and leather desk, the ventilation fan of a desktop computer hummed quietly.

"Copper," remarked Inspector Constable, "it really is uncommonly considerate of Mr. Cope to leave his computer on for us."

"He's on broadband, sir," replied Copper. "Not worth switching it off. You might almost think he knew we were coming."

"Under which circumstances," said the inspector, "it would be rude not to take a look and see what's on it. If only it weren't completely illegal and against all your training. You'd better hope I never find out."

"Right, sir." Sergeant Copper seated himself at the desk. "Mind you, guv, I'm probably on a hiding to nothing. I can't imagine that he hasn't used a password."

"Then you must just do your best, mustn't you, sergeant."

"I'll just try a few of the obvious ones, sir. You never know." Copper clicked various combinations of numbers and letters, without success. "I could be here all day."

"How hard can it be, sergeant? You're the one who did the computer course. All you have to do is start at the beginning of the alphabet and carry on through with every word in the English language until you get to Z."

"Hang on, sir." Dave Copper typed a word, pressed the return key, and burst out laughing. "I don't believe it! I must be psychic!" The computer screen flowered into action in front of him.

Andy Constable was impressed. "Well done, Copper. And the magic word is ...?"

"Zodiac, sir. It was the only word I could think of offhand that starts with Z."

"Right, sergeant, as you are now the expert, over to you. Any suggestions?"

"We could have a glance at his emails, sir." More clicks. "There's one new one in his Inbox from this morning."

"Go ahead."

"Now that's interesting, sir. It's about one of our suspects. It's from the editor of the Daily Stir. Listen to this ... 'Dear Horace, I was very interested to hear from you about sourcing prophecies on the internet. Not quite sure how this is relevant to The Stir, as we have our own resident clairvoyant, Seymour Cummings, as you know. However, since you say you will be in London next week, and as you seem to feel quite strongly that we should discuss the matter, please call my secretary to arrange an appointment. Signed, Kelvin Hastings.' What do you make of that, sir? Was our Mr. Cope stirring it up

63

for Mr. Cummings, do you reckon?"

"It does have that look about it," replied the inspector. "We shall have to have another word with Mr. Cummings, I think. Right, you carry on having a wander about in the computer, I'll see if there's anything in his paperwork."

Andy Constable turned his attention to a correspondence folder lying alongside the computer. There were copies of letters accepting invitations to literary lunches, gushing requests to deliver lectures at meetings of psychic investigation societies and spiritualist churches, and lists from publishing companies giving details of forthcoming works, accompanied by unsubtle expressions of hope that a favourable write-up might appear in Horace Cope's column. One letter, from the Family Records Office at Kew, puzzled him slightly. Obviously in response to an enquiry received from Horace Cope, it referred to an enclosed copy of a certificate of marriage between an Alexandra Justine Thyme and a Rex Lawler Biding, but although the receipt for the charge levied was stapled to the letter, the certificate itself was nowhere to be seen. The letter also stated that the Records Office had been unable to locate the register entry for the death of Rex Lawler Biding on the information provided.

"Copper," said Inspector Constable, "let's see if you can bring your fine police brain to bear on this." He read the letter to his colleague. "Who on earth are Alexandra Thyme and Rex Biding, and what was Horace Cope doing trying to find out about them? And where's that certificate?"

"I suppose the only thing we can do is ask Laura Biding, sir," replied the sergeant. "He's obviously some relation of hers. Maybe Horace Cope was doing some family research for her. She said he was an old close friend of the Lawdowns. Perhaps she's got it."

"Hmm." Andy Constable was not convinced. "Or maybe it's in that safe. But what would it be doing in there if it's for Laura? It just smells odd, and I don't know why." He put it to one side in his mind. "Anything else on the computer?"

"Nothing that jumps out at me, sir. Oh, hang on - there's an icon here for a photos file. It's just captioned 'L'. As in ..."

"As in that cutting in Mr. Cope's wallet." Constable smiled. "Well, don't just sit there, Copper - let's take a look."

A series of clicks followed. Dave Copper sighed. "Sorry, sir. Password protected, and it's not the same password as before. I could keep looking, but I don't really know what we're looking for, do I?"

The inspector made up his mind. "You're absolutely right. Shut it down, and we'll just have to rely on good old-fashioned detective work. Let's have a look in the desk drawer, and then we'll get out of here and get back to the Hall. We might get a few more answers up there." He pulled open the drawer. Among a clutter of paper clips, rubber bands, pencils, and a stapler, there nestled a fat brown padded envelope. Inside lay a thick hard-back book whose brightly-coloured dust-jacket seemed to follow a familiar pattern.

"Well, well," remarked Inspector Constable. "Now there's a surprise. 'Carrie Otter and the Deadly Pillows', eh? Who'd have thought it? I seem to remember Miss Highwater told us that Horace Cope wasn't too impressed with her Carrie Otter books, and here he is with one of them stashed away in his desk. Do you suppose he was a closet fan? Come on, Copper, this is more your area than mine. You know all about these books. So is this one of the good ones, or what?"

"Hang about, sir," answered Sergeant Copper. "This is the new one. Don't you remember, Miss Highwater told us that this was the last one, but it doesn't even come out till next month. There's been a great big publicity campaign about the launch, because it's the final book in the series and the publishers have been desperate to keep the press away from it in case they find out what happens. They've always done it every time there's a new one out - I reckon they just do it to bump up the sales."

"So how come Horace Cope has got a copy?"

"I expect Miss Highwater gave him an early copy so's he could do a write-up, sir. I mean, she did say she'd give me a signed copy."

"Yet another question I need an answer to. Let's get back to the Hall and start rattling a few cages. For a start, I want to talk to the vicar. I've lost count of the number of times that the first person to find a murder victim just happens to be the last person who saw them alive."

"But why would the vicar want Horace Cope dead?"

asked Dave Copper.

"That, sergeant," responded Andy Constable grimly, "is what I intend to find out."

Chapter 6

The sunlit promise of the day had vanished. Dammett Hall had developed a forlorn air in the thin drizzle which had started to fall as the detectives drew up outside the front door, and the strings of coloured bunting decorating the facade of the building hung limply. A few hunched figures could be seen scuttling to their cars and vans clutching boxes of ceramic dragons and armfuls of hand-knitted cardigans. A scattered handful of somewhat bedraggled boy scouts were collecting litter in black bin-bags. The village constable still stood at the top of the steps, slightly damp but exuding keenness.

"Well, Collins, anything to report?" asked the inspector.

"No sir, nothing really," answered the young officer. "You've just missed the van, sir. They've taken Mr. Cope away, and I think SOCO have finished inside as well, because they went about ten minutes ago. Some of the people from the village have been clearing their stalls and leaving, but I thought you wouldn't mind that so I let 'em go ahead and do it. I hope I did right, sir, but as you hadn't said anything, I reckoned it'd be all right. But everybody else is still in the house like you said."

"Good man. I'll be inside questioning the suspects, if anyone wants me."

"Actually, sir ..."

"Yes, Collins?"

"There was somebody who wanted a word, sir. Mr. Porter ... Gideon Porter ... he owns the Dammett Well Inn. That's the pub in the village. He said he had a couple of things you might want to know about. He's over there in the beer tent."

"Reliable, is he?" put in Sergeant Copper. "I've met a few pub landlords in my time that I wouldn't trust as far as I could throw them."

Collins laughed. "I don't think you ought to try that with old Gideon, sergeant, if you don't mind me saying so. He must weigh about eighteen stone. But he's as honest as you like. He's never so much as offered me a free pint, so you can take that as you may. I'd trust him."

"Thank you, Collins," responded the inspector. "We'd

better have a word with him."

The beer tent stood by the garden wall close to the gate which Constable surmised led through to the Secret Garden where Horace Cope's booth had been set up. Gideon Porter was just finishing stacking a pile of beer-crates as the detectives entered the tent. He mopped a pink and perspiring face as they introduced themselves, and moved behind a trestle table obviously intended to serve as a bar, where several rotating optics stood dismantled.

"I'm glad you're here, gents," he declared. "Young Robbie Collins told you I had a couple of snippets for you, did he? Only I thought I ought to tell you, because you never know, do you? I don't suppose either of you fancies a drink while you're here, before I put these away? No, of course not - not while you're on duty." He smiled roguishly as both detectives shook their heads. "Sure I can't tempt you? No? Oh well. I think I will, if you don't mind. That's the advantage of running a pub, see. You can always have a bit of a noggin in times of stress." He poured himself a generous whisky.

"Bit stressed, are we, sir?" enquired Dave Copper.

"Well, who wouldn't be?" replied Gideon. "This business with Horace is pretty ghastly, you got to admit."

"So, you were a friend of Mr. Cope's then, Mr. Porter?" asked Andy Constable.

"Ah. Well." Gideon shifted awkwardly. "I wouldn't go so far as to say we were actually friends, but I knew him quite well because he came into my pub a lot. Mind you, everybody in the village does at some time or another, so I don't suppose that tells you anything."

"So you wouldn't say you were close?"

"Lord, no, anything but. No, that's not fair. In my business you get the habit of getting on with everybody. But to be frank, he wasn't really my sort of bloke. Don't get me wrong - he was always pleasant enough to me, but I always got the feeling he wasn't quite as nice as he made out."

Constable's interest was aroused. "What makes you say that, Mr. Porter?"

"Well, inspector, …" Gideon took a deep breath. "You might laugh, but I reckon being a pub landlord is a bit like being a priest. You know, the secrets of the confessional and so on, if you get my drift. People say stuff, and they don't always pay too much attention to who's listening. I'm not normally one to repeat things, but I suppose this murder business makes it a bit different. Now you take the other day. Horace came into the pub with that cousin of his, Albert. Do you know him?"

"Oh yes," put in Dave Copper. "We've met Mr. Ross. We had quite an interesting interview with him earlier."

"Ah. Well then, you've probably got a bit of an idea what he's like." Gideon chuckled. "It's not funny really, but we all call him the Human Sponge - I don't think I've ever seen him buy his own drink. He always got Horace to pay - well, either Horace or anyone else who happened to be standing there at the time. He ain't too fussed."

"Now I should have thought that would put people's backs up, wouldn't you, sergeant?"

"Not any more," answered Gideon. "It might have at first, but Albert's done it to so many people that it's a bit of a standing joke with my regulars. It's quite comical - Albert comes in on his own, and they all start shuffling up the other end of the bar so's not to get caught."

"And was Horace in on the joke?"

"Lord, no. You daren't say anything to Horace - he'd have been up in the air about it straight away. He had a bit of a temper on him sometimes."

Andy Constable felt that the conversation seemed to be straying from the point. "So what has this got to do with what you were saying about the other day?"

"Ah, well, that's the whole thing, you see," explained Gideon. "Now that particular day, Horace was in one of his bad moods, so that's how I come heard what I did."

"Which was ...?"

"Well, Horace and Albert were stood at one end of the bar, and Horace was hissing on something about 'not putting up any longer', and then Albert said 'But what do I do? Where do I go?', and Horace said he didn't really give a damn, pardon the language, and he said Albert had a week to sort it out, or else." Gideon paused for breath.

"So not a particularly cousinly conversation then, Mr. Porter? Any ideas on what it was all about?"

Gideon pulled a wry face. "Well, there is a bit of

69

background there. I might be wrong, but I don't reckon Horace trusted Albert one little bit, for all that he was family."

"And what makes you say that?"

"You see, Horace had been going on to anyone who would listen about this new TV show he was going to be on - well, so he said, although I think Seymour Cummings had other ideas. Anyway, Horace was telling people how he would be spending a lot more time away in London, and I think he wanted Albert out of the cottage before he went."

Dave Copper looked up from his notebook. "Now why do you think he would want that, sir? When we spoke to Mr. Ross, we got the impression that he was looking after Mr. Cope's cottage while he was staying there, as some sort of unpaid housekeeper."

"Hmm, that's as may be," responded Gideon. "Now Robbie Collins says you've been up at the cottage, so you know better than me what it's like. I've never been in there meself, but talk is it's all a bit ..." He paused as if in search of the right word.

"Exotic?" suggested the inspector with a slight smile.

"Aah, you may be right. I wouldn't like to judge. So anyway, what with Horace being very nicely off, thank you, which he never made a secret of, and him being a bit ... arty, so to speak, we all knew that he had quite a few pretty nice bits and pieces up there. But from what I can gather, there have been some of his antiques go missing - really valuable Georgian silver and paintings and suchlike. He was a bit of a collector by all accounts, was our Horace."

Andy Constable raised an eyebrow. "Missing, you say?"

"That's right - missing," retorted Gideon in heavy tones. "It was all put down to a burglary, but if you ask me, it didn't quite add up. Course, they had Robbie Collins in, but he never got anywhere with it. Nice enough boy, but when all's said and done, he's just the village bobby. He's not a professional like you gents. But I reckon Horace had found out something and he suspected Albert of pinching his things and selling them off, and that's what the row was all about. Not that it would surprise me. Since he lost all his money in shares and stuff, Albert's never had two ha'pennies to rub together, poor sod."

"Yes sir," said Dave Copper. "Mr. Ross told us about his

run of bad luck before he moved down here from London."

"London!" Gideon smacked his forehead. "That was the other thing! Good job you said that, sergeant, else I'd have forgotten. That's my trouble, you see. I get talking, and stuff goes clean out of my head."

"So?" enquired Constable. "London?"

"London!" repeated Gideon in meaningful tones. "That's another thing I overheard a nice little snippet about. Here, inspector, you could do your crime statistics a power of good, you know." He chuckled. "You ever want to know anything, you just come and stand in my pub for a bit."

"So tell us about this snippet?"

"Right you are. So, the other day ... ooh, must have been last week sometime, I suppose. It had gone a bit quiet, and there wasn't anyone else in at the time, so I was having a chat to Robin Allday ... I expect you know him? The solicitor?"

"Yes," said Constable. "We know Mr. Allday. In fact, we've already had a word with him this morning. Why, is there something else that he may be able to help us with?"

"Well, of course, it may all be nothing to do with anything, and I wouldn't want to stir things up for Robin, being as he's a good bloke and a good customer and all."

"Why don't you just tell us what it is and leave us to be the judge?" suggested the inspector gently. "If it's not relevant, we can quite easily forget anything you tell us. So, you were having a chat about ...?"

"Oh, just this and that, really, nothing special, but anyway, we got on to property prices. Course, they're all over the papers at the moment, and Robin knows all there is to know round here, 'cos he does all the conveyancing and suchlike, that is if there is any, you know what the market is, and it was saying in the paper the other day that they don't know whether it's all going to go up or down, so I'm just glad I inherited the pub from my old dad cos I ain't got to worry about that sort of thing, except of course for the smoking business which hasn't done me a lot of good, but I suppose you have to put up with these sorts of things ... now, where was I?"

"Property."

"Ah, that's right. So there we were, just chatting like, and in comes Horace and he walks up to the bar, and he obviously heard what we were saying, and he says, 'Ah, Robin. Property. That's just what I want a quiet word with you about, if you don't mind, Gideon.' And I thought, 'Alright, squire, I can take a hint,' so I got on with clearing up a few glasses down the other end of the bar."

"So you didn't hear any more of what it was about?" asked Constable.

"Ah, well, see, inspector, that's just where you're wrong." Gideon had the grace to look faintly embarrassed. "I did hear. I don't know why, but I thought there was something in his manner, if you get me. Horace's, that is. And also there was the fact that he obviously didn't want me to hear, and I got to admit I'm as curious as the next man. Well, it's only human nature, isn't it? So there I was thinking 'What's he up to?', so I listened in a bit when they weren't paying attention."

"So if I could just make a note of what it was that Mr. Cope wanted to talk to Mr. Allday about," suggested Dave Copper.

Gideon grew a little pinker. "Honestly, I don't much like talking about people behind their backs, gents. There's some dreadful gossips in this village, which I don't hold with. Now a bit of harmless chat, that's one thing, but repeating confidential stuff - well, that's different. I wouldn't normally do it, but I suppose as it's a question of murder ..."

Andy Constable adopted his most reassuring tones. "We can be very discreet, Mr. Porter," he coaxed. "If it's appropriate. So ..."

"Well, inspector, if you say so. It turns out that Horace is buying a flat in London - I don't know exactly where, cos I didn't hear that bit - and he wants Robin to do some sort of fiddle on the deeds to avoid paying stamp duty or something. And not only that, but there was something about putting it in someone else's name because of Capital Gains Tax."

Dave Copper beamed. "I love it. Now that is a very juicy bit of fraud, isn't it sir? That's about the first definite bit of motive we've come up with. I can see that we're going to have to have another nice long conversation with Mr. Allday."

"Let's not be too hasty, sergeant," replied the inspector. "Don't forget. Mr. Cope might have intended to buy this flat and engage in this fiddle that Mr. Porter mentions, but he certainly won't be going ahead with his purchase now, will he? And in case it's slipped your mind, the doctor's got Mr. Cope down at the mortuary, so it won't be too easy questioning him on the subject, will it? Plus there's the matter of hearsay evidence - I don't know that the courts would be too keen on relying on Mr. Porter's eaves-droppings."

Dave Copper's face fell a little, and Gideon Porter hurried to join in. "Hold on, because you didn't let me finish. That wasn't the end of it. See, Horace stood there looking smug, cos that was always his way anyway, but then Robin said he was a professional man, and he couldn't do that sort of thing, and then Horace said 'I don't see why not, you've done it often enough before for other people'."

"And how did Mr. Allday respond to that?" asked Constable.

"Well," said Gideon, "he just spluttered a bit, and Horace looked even smugger, and he said to Robin 'Well, think it over. But it's not going to do your career a lot of good if it gets out, is it?', and then off he went."

"So what happened then?"

"Course, I couldn't say anything, could I, being as how I wasn't supposed to have heard all of this. So I just quietly slipped Robin a large brandy - he looked as if he needed it, just sitting there a bit taken aback like."

"And in your opinion, could there be any truth in what Mr. Cope had said?"

"I honestly couldn't say," asserted Gideon firmly. "Robin's always been perfectly straight with me, so I take as I find."

"And he didn't say anything at the time?"

"Not a word, inspector. And I didn't want to hover round him, so I popped down the cellar to get another crate of light ale up, and by the time I got back in the bar he'd drunk up and gone."

"And have you seen him since? Or Mr. Cope, for that matter? Was anything further said on the subject?"

"Course I've seen Robin. He pops in most days - he was in yesterday, and I said I'd most probably see him up here. I cracked some joke about him getting Horace to tell his fortune, which he didn't seem to find all that funny. He said he reckoned

Horace knew too much about people already. But Horace - no, I don't think I've seen him since. No, I tell a lie - I saw him go past with Albert while I was finishing setting up here, so that must have been around twelve-ish, but I was busy, and he didn't speak. Lord ..." He seemed struck by the thought. "That'd be the last time I saw him alive." He shook his head. "You just never know, do you?"

"Indeed you don't, Mr. Porter," agreed Constable. "So, if that's all you can tell us, I don't think we need to keep you any longer. You've obviously got your work cut out here."

"Oh, don't fret about that, inspector," smiled Gideon. "I got my two lads coming up from the village to get it all on the truck. We'll have it done in a jiffy. To tell you the truth, the sooner I get back to the pub, the better. I got the feeling that tonight's going to be pretty busy, what with this business with Horace. There's nothing my customers like more than a good chin-wag about a bit of local goings-on, and it don't get much better than this. If you see what I mean, and no disrespect to Horace, rest his soul."

As he turned to go, a thought occurred to the Inspector.

"Just one thing, Mr. Porter. That little wooden gate just outside ...?"

"The one through to the Secret Garden? What about it?"

"Did you notice anyone go through it after Horace Cope arrived?"

Gideon scratched his head in thought. "I can't say as I did, but mind you, I wasn't paying that much attention on account of I was getting everything sorted out here. But I don't see as how they could, because it's always kept locked as far as I know. Course, it was going to be open today so's people could go through and see Horace. Sorry, I don't suppose that helps, does it?"

"Not to worry, Mr. Porter. It was just a thought."

Chapter 7

As Constable and Copper re-entered the hall of the house, they almost collided with the scurrying figure of Amelia Cook as she emerged from the drawing room carrying an empty tray, leaving behind her cries of "So kind, Amelia", and "Thank the lord, I'm starving".

"Miss Cook, would it be?" enquired Constable. "We'd like a word, if we may ..."

"I can't stop - I'm up to my ears in the kitchen." And she disappeared at speed through the green baize door into the corridor, leaving the detectives to exchange amused glances before following her.

The kitchen of Dammett Hall was a show-piece of the Edwardian architect's art. Sparkling tiles of white and blue with interwoven art nouveau designs covered the walls to ceiling height, while along one side of the room an enormous cast-iron range with brass fittings offered a bewildering choice of oven doors, cooking plates, and water boilers. Shelves along another wall carried an impressive array of gleaming copper dishes and pans, while beneath the windows, which rose from above head height to the top of the room, a row of lead-lined sinks, interspersed with wooden draining boards, gave evidence that the scullery-maids of former days were not encouraged to gaze at the outside world as they worked. Discreetly placed, a modern range and refrigerator indicated that the room was not entirely for show. The centre of the room was dominated by a huge wooden table, scrubbed white, which at present was spread with baking trays, bags of flour and tubs of butter, china plates and dishes, and an incongruous pile of large tupperware containers. Amelia Cook stood at the head of the table, looking around as if uncertain what she should do next.

"Yes?" she said a touch crossly, pushing a strand of hair off her face with the back of a wrist. "What is it you want?"

"We're very sorry to have to interrupt you when you're obviously busy, madam," replied Andy Constable in his most soothing tones, "but I'm afraid it's official business. I'm Detective Inspector Constable - this is Sergeant Copper."

"Well, you should have said, shouldn't you?" Amelia took a deep breath and seemed to calm down a little. "I do apologise, Inspector. I'm sorry I'm a bit flustered, but I'm all at sixes and sevens at the moment, and I had to break off just now in the middle of some cream horns because Lady Lawdown wanted some sandwiches if you please, and you know what it's like if your rough puff goes flabby."

"I can imagine," smiled Constable. "But I'm afraid it's all rather more serious than that, of course. We do need to ask you some questions about the death of Horace Cope."

"Horace Cope? Horrid man! I didn't like him a bit."

Constable was taken aback at the sudden vehemence. "That's a very strong statement to make, madam. Do you mind telling us why?"

Amelia subsided on to one of the kitchen chairs surrounding the table, and after a moment, the two policemen did likewise. Discreetly, Dave Copper produced his notebook and opened it expectantly.

"Oh, no particular reason, I suppose," replied Amelia. "It's not as if he ever did anything to me. But I never could like the way he treated my friends - he seemed to have a knack of upsetting them. He was always making remarks in a meaningful tone, as if he was getting at people for some reason. He was just ... I don't know ...well, rather slimy in his manner. Of course, that's just my private opinion. I can't abide gossip, so you'll get nothing of that sort from me."

"Ah, but it's always helpful to hear what people really think of a murder victim, madam," remarked Constable. "We so rarely get to hear people's candid opinions."

Amelia sniffed dismissively. "Well, of course, one isn't supposed to speak ill of the dead, is one, Inspector? That's what they say. Especially with Horace Cope." She gave a little giggle. "You never know - being a psychic, he might come back and haunt me! Oh, what a dreadful thing to say! I really shouldn't joke at a time like this. Whatever will you think of me?" She resumed her serious manner. "So, how can I help you?"

"Copper?" Constable handed over to his colleague.

"I'm just making a note of who was where and when today, madam," said the sergeant. "If you can just help us to build up the picture..."

"I'm not sure I know anything at all, really," replied Amelia. "I've been here at the Hall all morning, but I've hardly set foot outside the kitchen. As for Mr. Cope, I haven't even clapped eyes on him, which is no wonder, considering everything I've had to do, and now look, it's really all been such a waste, which I honestly can't afford, so if you don't mind, I'd like to get on, because I want to be away from here and get back to the village, and Laura said I wasn't to leave until I'd spoken to you, so I thought, well, at least I can use the time to take advantage of this lovely big kitchen, because really, my kitchen at the Copper Kettle is just a cubby-hole compared to this, but for all that, I'd much rather be there than here ..."

"Just one second, madam." Copper managed to interrupt the flow. "We seem to be getting rather ahead of ourselves. Can we just go back to the start, please? Can you tell us how you came to be here at the Hall today in the first place? Do you work for Lady Lawdown?"

Before Amelia could reply, Andy Constable spoke. "I think if you check your notes, sergeant, you'll find that Miss Biding has already mentioned that Her Ladyship had engaged Miss Cook to do some catering for the fete. Isn't that right, madam?"

"That's right, inspector. I usually do it for Sandra, because although I say it as shouldn't, my little establishment has quite a reputation in the area, and I'm sure that some of the visitors come just for my cakes, but of course one doesn't like to presume, so I was quite pleased when Sandra asked me to do it again this year ... that must have been, ooh, about six weeks ago. Because, of course, I have to plan ahead, because the fete is always on a Saturday, and Saturday is usually quite a busy day for me for teas, so I have to close up, but I always make sure that I put notices up and do some leaflets telling my clientele that I'm going to be up here at the Hall on that day, because I hate to disappoint people."

"Yes, of course, madam," Constable managed to squeeze in.

Amelia was not to be stopped. "And now look what's happened! This horrible business with Horace, and please don't think I'm being unfeeling, because that's not like me at all, but the only thing I want to do now is to get back to the Copper

Kettle and open up and see if I can stop all my lovely food going to waste. It won't keep for ever, you know, especially not the sponges. But if I know my customers, there's nothing they enjoy more than a good gossip over a piece of cake and a cup of tea, and I'm usually open until seven on a Saturday. So if that's everything ...?" She made to rise.

Andy Constable decided to take control. "Actually, no, Miss Cook. We really must talk about Mr. Cope. So the sooner we can do that, the sooner we can let you go. So if you wouldn't mind ..."

"Oh. Very well, inspector." Amelia subsided on to her chair once more. "Ask away."

"I think you said that you hadn't seen Mr. Cope at all today, is that right?"

"That is correct, inspector. I arrived here long before anyone else this morning, and I don't think the others got here until about mid-day, from what I've heard."

"So when would be the last time you actually did see Mr. Cope?"

"Ooh, let me think - when was it? I think it must have been last week some time. Yes, that's right, because he came into the Copper Kettle with Helen Highwater one morning for coffee and cake. I remember, because that day I'd done one of my special rich fruit cakes." She turned to Sergeant Copper. "Have you tried my special rich fruit cake, sergeant? No? Now, you really must. You look to me like a boy who likes his cakes. I'll cut you a piece in a second when we've finished."

"I'm sure Sergeant Copper would like that very much," put in Andy Constable, "but I think we're straying from the point again. You were saying ...?"

"Was I? Oh yes, Horace and Helen. Yes, I was quite surprised to see them together, because they're not normally what you'd think of as chums, but I saw them outside just before they came in, and I got the impression that Horace had button-holed her so that he could speak to her about something."

Sergeant Copper's pencil poised itself over his notebook. "Would you by any chance have an idea of what it was, madam?"

Amelia drew herself up slightly. "I do hope you're not

78

implying that I would eavesdrop on my customers' conversations, sergeant."

"Not at all, madam," replied Copper calmly. "But sometimes it's impossible not to hear what people are saying, especially if you're close to them."

"That's true, sergeant," said Amelia, mollified. "Of course, I was to and fro to the table, and serving other customers, so I didn't hear a great deal of what went on, but I do know that it was about her books - you know, the Carrie Otter series."

"Yes," sighed Andy Constable. "We've already had a couple of conversations about young Miss Otter's adventures - haven't we, sergeant?"

"Oh, are you a Carrie Otter fan as well, sergeant?" beamed Amelia. "I certainly am. I've read them all - they're very good, aren't they? Well, I think so, but then, of course, I'm no intellectual - not like Horace. Or so he thought, with his book reviews in the Sunday paper. I'm not at all sure Horace would have agreed with me - not after what he said in his column about the last one." She sniffed.

"And can you remember what he did say, Miss Cook?" enquired the inspector.

"I can, inspector, because I remember reading the write-up in the paper and getting quite hot under the collar. He had the cheek to call it 'Carrie Otter and the Half-Baked Plot', he said that anyone with half a brain would enjoy the story because they wouldn't need the other half, and he described the whole book as ... now, what did he call it? Oh yes - 'A load of old warlocks'!" Sergeant Copper suddenly seemed highly engrossed in the contents of his notebook, and emitted a swiftly-suppressed choking sound.

"But that was Horace Cope all over," continued Amelia. "He fancied himself very much above the Common Man. I call it most unnecessary and most unkind, and I believe Helen was quite upset about it at the time. But obviously she must have forgiven him, because there they were having coffee together. It just goes to show you never can tell, doesn't it?"

Andy Constable made a further effort to steer Amelia's ramblings back to the investigation. "So what did you happen to hear of their conversation last week?"

"Well, I think Helen was trying to persuade Horace to be a bit nicer about her next book. She was saying how exciting it was all going to be, and she was really being very enthusiastic and talking about how much her fans were looking forward to it. In fact, she asked him if he would like a copy to look at as a special favour, and he just waved the idea away. 'No need, my dear, no need,' he said, and Helen sounded a bit taken aback and said 'Oh. Very well'. I thought Horace sounded very patronising, but I don't think Helen noticed. I suppose she was trying to talk him around to how most people feel about her books."

"And how did Mr. Cope respond to her efforts?"

"I didn't quite hear it all, because I was making a cappuccino for someone, and that coffee machine does make such a noise, which is not at all in keeping with the sort of atmosphere I like to cultivate at the Copper Kettle, but of course these days some of the modern customers seem to have developed quite a taste for these coffees with continental names - it's all these foreign holidays, you see - so I have to be able to do those as well as a nice traditional filter coffee. So ... now, where was I?"

"You were telling us what Mr. Cope said," answered Constable with a patient smile which was beginning to grow rather fixed.

"Ah, yes. Well, that's the annoying thing. I'm sure it must have been something important, because of the way Helen reacted, but I'm not sure I heard him properly because the coffee machine chose that moment to make one of its horrid spluttering sounds. Horace said something about somebody's mother - no, 'getting mothered', that was it."

"'Mothered?' Who was getting mothered? And who by?"

"No, wait a minute - that's not right, but it was something like that." Amelia gazed at the ceiling and flipped her fingers in frustration. "Oh, it's so irritating when you can't remember, isn't it, inspector?"

"Quite so, madam," replied Constable, stifling a sigh.

Amelia beamed brightly. "Oh, don't you worry, inspector," she trilled. "It'll come to me. These things always do. Usually when I'm in the middle of getting something out of the oven, and I can't do anything about them."

"Well, do let us know if you remember."

"I will, inspector, never fear. Anyway, whatever it was, Helen looked quite shocked and asked what on earth he meant."

"And what do you think he meant?" asked Copper.

"I haven't the faintest idea, sergeant," replied Amelia with a tone of baffled triumph. "I didn't hear it properly, did I? But then he went on to say that he had friends in the printing business, and that he was sure that she knew all about publishers' advances, if she knew what he meant."

"And did he ... she?" asked Copper, who by this time was becoming hopelessly confused by Amelia's tangled syntax.

"Well, obviously she did, because she glared at Horace and said 'Don't you dare!', and then he said 'It's all a question of whether it's worth more to you than it is to me. Your readers or mine?'."

"And what was Miss Highwater's response to that, Miss Cook?" enquired the inspector, taking pity on his colleague, who was scribbling frantically.

"Nothing, inspector. She just picked up her bag, got to her feet without another word, and left in a great hurry. Never even said goodbye to me, which is most unlike Helen. And, she didn't even touch her Viennese Fancy, and I've never known that to happen before."

Inspector Constable exchanged glances with Sergeant Copper. "It sounds, Miss Cook, as if the Copper Kettle is the place to come if one wants to witness a little excitement in Dammett Worthy," he remarked. "It seems you had quite an eventful morning."

Amelia Cook raised an eyebrow at the detective. "Now you're making fun of me, inspector," she said, "but as it happens, you haven't heard the full story."

"So there's more?"

"Indeed, there is, inspector, if the sergeant has his notebook quite ready." Amelia settled herself back in her chair, her earlier urgency seemingly forgotten, along with her disinclination to gossip.

"Go on."

Amelia drew a deep breath. "Well, I don't suppose it could have been more than a minute or two after Helen left, because Horace was still sitting there looking pleased with himself, and Laura Biding came in. So Horace looked up, smiled at her with that oily smile of his when he wanted something, and said 'Come and sit with me, Laura. Let me treat you to a coffee. I've got a little business proposition to put to you.' There was just something in his tone - I thought to myself, 'I don't like the sound of that'."

"And ... er ... did you by any chance ...?"

"Oh sergeant, don't be silly - of course I listened in. Laura's a dear girl, and for all that the family has known Horace for years and Laura has always called him 'Uncle', I still didn't like Horace's tone."

"And what did this 'business proposition' turn out to be?" asked the inspector.

"Well, that's the thing, inspector. I'm still not quite sure. Horace was so ... I suppose 'oblique' is the word. He said something about Laura coming up to see him in his new flat in London, and she said she didn't know if she could, and then he said he'd got a wonderful collection of photographs, and they could go through them together and see if she thought any of them were particularly interesting."

"Photographs? What sort of photographs?"

"He didn't say, inspector. Of course, Laura has done some modelling work for the smart magazines, so I expect it could have been something to do with that. Anyway, he just said that some of the pictures were 'quite arresting'." Amelia sounded perplexed. "I thought it seemed a funny thing to say when he said it, but then of course I was off to the kitchen again to toast some teacakes, and then it went clean out of my mind."

"You didn't find any photographs at Mr. Cope's cottage, did you, Copper?" enquired Constable.

"Not a thing, sir," replied Copper. "Mind you, he might have had something on that computer of his - I didn't get a chance to have a real go at that. And then there was the safe - we might find something in there. If we knew what we were looking for."

"Yes, sergeant. Well, we'll just have to wait until we've got the search warrant, won't we," said Constable briskly. "So did Mr. Cope not explain about these photographs?"

"Not that I heard, inspector."

"And what about Miss Biding? How did she react to these remarks of Mr. Cope's?"

Amelia leaned forward and dropped her voice. "Well, that's the thing, inspector. She didn't say anything at all. Of course, I couldn't see her face, because she was sitting with her back to me facing the window, but I got the impression that she just sort of froze. Anyway, by the time I came back into the tearoom, Horace was saying something about her using his flat for business, and I remember he said 'it was a good game, but he knew a better one'. He was smiling all over that horrid shiny face of his as if it was the greatest joke, but I must say that Laura didn't seem to find it very funny."

"No?"

"Not at all, inspector. Ah, but then she did speak up. She said something about Lady Lawdown having the influence to get him stopped, and Horace just scoffed. He said he knew all about that, and that he had the proof, and it wasn't as if she was that much of a lady anyway. Honestly, that made my blood boil. When I think of how much Lady Lawdown does for this village and all her work as a magistrate and everything, and of how nice she's been to Horace over the years, it was just so two-faced of him to say that. I don't know why Laura didn't just slap his face. Both of them!"

"It certainly doesn't sound like the friendliest of comments," remarked Constable.

"It made me quite hot under the collar, inspector," said Amelia, her feathers obviously thoroughly ruffled at the mere memory. "But of course I couldn't say anything because they would have known I was listening to a private conversation, and that would never do, would it?"

"Not at all, madam. So what happened after that?"

"Well ... nothing, I'm afraid." Amelia seem conscious of a slight anticlimax. "Horace just got up, came up to the counter and paid me in the most patronising way, and slithered out, leaving Laura just sitting there gazing out of the window. I went over to collect the empty cups and she didn't even seem to notice I was there, and I didn't like to say anything, and then she left a few minutes afterwards."

"And that was the last time you saw him?" asked Copper, turning over yet another page of his rapidly-filling notebook.

"Yes. Oh! No! I tell a lie!"

"Well, now, you wouldn't want to lie to the police, would you, madam?"

"Of course not, sergeant. But that wasn't the last time I saw Horace. Of course, I don't know whether it matters ..."

"You never know when this information is going to be helpful, madam," coaxed Copper. "So when was it then?"

"It was the other day ... it must have been Tuesday. I was on my way to the church, because I do the flowers every second Tuesday and every third Friday, and it was my turn, although I'm sure that if I didn't mark it on the calendar I'd never be there at the right time. All of us in the Flower Society do our bit to help out, and the vicar is such a dear sweet man, and it must have come as an awful shock to him, finding Horace the way he did, but you know what they say, 'In the midst of life, we are in death', although I'm sure Mr. Pugh didn't expect to have to take the Bible quite so literally ... or is it the Book of Common Prayer ...?" Amelia tailed off and looked expectantly at the detectives. "I don't suppose you remember which, do you?"

Inspector Constable shook himself slightly. "Be that as it may, Miss Cook, I think you were going to tell us when you saw Mr. Cope."

"Oh. Yes. Silly me. Well, it was then. Horace was walking up the lane from the church just as I arrived. I didn't speak to him, though."

"So that was all, was it?" The inspector was disappointed.

"Yes, I'm afraid so, inspector. I did the flowers while the bell-ringing practice was going on, and I hadn't quite finished when it ended, and I came past the vestry door, and Lady Lawdown was in there looking through some papers."

"With anyone else?"

"I don't think so. I didn't see anyone, but then, most of the bell-ringers go out of the small side door at the bottom of the tower, so I wouldn't normally see them. I expect the vicar was about somewhere, because I'd seen him earlier on, but I hadn't really been paying much attention because I was concentrating on making the flowers nice."

"So you didn't actually speak to anyone at all?"

"Well, only to say 'Evening, Your Ladyship!' Poor Sandra,

I must have taken her quite by surprise, because she jumped like a startled ferret, bundled something into her handbag, and was off like a shot! It was quite funny, really. So then I just topped up the water in all the vases and came home, by which time of course Horace was long gone. So I really do think that's all I can tell you."

Inspector Constable let out a long breath. "We're very grateful, madam. I'm sure we shall find the copious notes which my sergeant has taken most enlightening." He raised his eyebrows invitingly at Dave Copper.

"Absolutely, sir. I'm sure I've got everything."

"Then we'll leave you to get on with it, Miss Cook. Thank you once again. Come along, Copper."

"It's no trouble, inspector," warbled Amelia. "If there's anything else you want to know, please don't hesitate to ask. You can always find me at the Copper Kettle. Oh, sergeant ..." Her hand went to her mouth. "I've been talking on, and I never got you your piece of cake."

"I'll ... er ... I'll have it another time, madam," spluttered Copper, and the two detectives escaped into the corridor.

"Good lord, can she talk?" gasped Dave Copper, flexing the fingers of his writing hand.

"Quite so, sergeant," responded Andy Constable, "which is why I shut you up on the subject of trawling through Horace Cope's computer and safe. The last thing I want to do is to create the impression with someone who is obviously one of Dammett Worthy's keenest gossips that we do not stick carefully to official procedures. So watch it."

"Sorry, sir," said Copper. "Still, you can't beat a bit of gossip for finding out stuff about people, can you? Sounds as if Miss Laura Biding has got some sort of secret, doesn't it?"

"Not just her, by the sound of it. What do you make of that business about Helen Highwater's book, or Lady Lawdown fiddling about in the church? I think they've all got some sort of secret lurking in there. Ah well, it makes our job that much more interesting, I suppose. Right then, sergeant. Let's see what else we can find out. Onward and upward!"

Chapter 8

Back in the hall, Dave Copper turned to Andy Constable. "What next, then, sir?"

"Who rather than what, I think, sergeant. We're overdue for a chat with the vicar, if he's back in the land of the living. So let's find out where they've put him." He knocked on the door of the drawing room and led the way in. Six faces turned to him expectantly.

Lady Lawdown rose and crossed the room briskly towards the detectives. "Dear inspector, I do hope you aren't going to keep us penned up in here all day. Have you managed to sort out this horrible business yet?"

Andy Constable smiled. "I'm sorry, your ladyship, but I'm afraid these things take a little longer than that. But I think we're making progress. But in the meantime, I'm afraid I'm going to have to ask everyone to stay put for a little longer, if you don't mind. I know Miss Cook has managed to keep you supplied with provisions, and I'm sure you're not too uncomfortable in here. At least it's a lot cosier than the police station."

Lady Lawdown looked shocked. "The police station?" she echoed. "Do you mean ... Are you seriously telling me that we are suspects? For heaven's sake, man, look at us!"

Five pairs of eyes declined to meet the inspector's.

"I'm saying exactly that, I'm afraid, your ladyship, unless and until I have better information which rules some or all of you out."

"But that's ludicrous!" retorted Lady Lawdown. "Why on earth would any of us have the slightest reason to murder Horace Cope? It's far more likely to have been some hooligan from one of the other villages. I have them up in front of me all the time in the magistrates' court. That's it - it's some sort of mugging or robbery, and someone's got carried away."

"That, I think, is one motive we can rule out," replied Constable. "As for others ... well, we shall just have to continue to investigate. Which leads me to my next question - can you tell me where the vicar is? I need to find out what he can tell

86

us."

Lady Lawdown seemed to calm down a little. "Of course, inspector. Poor dear man, I hope he's feeling up to speaking to you."

"You worry too much, Sandra," interposed Seymour Cummings. "The old boy's been in the village for donkey's years. I should think there isn't much he hasn't seen. He's a tough old bird, inspector. I think you'll be surprised."

Lady Lawdown looked unconvinced. "If you say so, Seymour. Laura, I think he's in the Chinese Bedroom, isn't he, darling? Show the gentlemen the way, would you. It seems the rest of us had better stay here, as the inspector insists. I think I need to make a telephone call."

"If you'd just lead on, miss," said Constable, standing aside for Laura. He paused at the door. "By the way, your ladyship, if it's not too much of an inconvenience, I'd be glad if you didn't make any telephone calls just for the moment." He turned to Dave Copper and muttered under his breath as they left the room, "Especially not to the Chief Constable." The door closed behind them.

At the head of the stairs, Laura Biding turned left and led the way along a short corridor. She tapped on a door and put her head around it. "Only me, Mr. Pugh. How are you feeling?" she asked, and in response to the murmured reply, stood back to let the officers into the room. "I'll be downstairs, inspector, with the others," she said, and disappeared towards the hall.

The curtains to the Chinese Bedroom were partially drawn, lending the room an atmosphere of gloom. In the twilight, exotic richly-coloured birds flew among groves of bamboo overlooking a distant river disappearing into a gorge between misty blue mountains, while in the undergrowth, golden pheasants strutted with a haughty air. Around the room, spindly bamboo chairs alternated with heavily-lacquered elaborately carved cabinets in sombre shades of red and gold. Fretted black wooden screens partially concealed a huge bed draped in heavily-embroidered silk curtains. And, small and huddled into insignificance in the centre of the bed, the grey-suited figure of the Reverend Ivor Pugh. The vicar struggled into a sitting position and turned his pale face towards the detectives. A faint aroma of whisky surrounded him.

"I'm really sorry to have to disturb you, sir." Inspector Constable was at his most soothing.

"No, no, please do come in ... inspector, did Laura say?"

"That's right, sir. I'm Detective Inspector Constable, and this is Sergeant Copper. I know you've had something of an unsettling experience, but I'm afraid we do need to find out what you can tell us about Mr. Cope's death."

"No, inspector, I quite understand," replied the vicar, swinging his legs over the side of the bed and visibly appearing to concentrate his mind. "One has to do one's duty, and you must ask your questions, and I'll do my best to answer them. I'm just sorry I wasn't able to speak to you sooner, but it was ...well, you know, the shock. Finding Horace like that. I suppose when you've lived in the world as long as I have, you should be used to all sorts of things, but when you see something like that ..." His voice tailed off, and his gaze became unfocussed.

"We have seen Mr. Cope's body, Mr. Pugh, so we can appreciate that it would have been deeply unpleasant when you discovered him, so we'll cover that as quickly as we can. How did it come about exactly?"

Ivor Pugh collected his thoughts. "I'd arrived to open the fete as arranged with Lady Lawdown," he said, "and I think I was one of the first to arrive. Oh no - I believe Helen was here before me." He turned to Dave Copper who had seated himself gingerly on one of the bamboo chairs to the side of the bed. "That's Helen Highwater, sergeant."

"That's perfectly alright, sir," replied Copper. "We have met the others, so we know who everyone is. Do carry on."

"Lady Lawdown had arranged a little drinks party beforehand as she usually does, but I expect you know that already," resumed the vicar. "Twelve o'clock, she said, because I was due to open the fete at one. It's all in aid of the church roof, you know. Well, I say all, but of course Lady Lawdown and I have an arrangement to share the proceeds. I honestly couldn't tell you whose roof is more in need of repair, you know - hers or mine! But that's all by the by - I'm sure you don't want to be bothered by such matters. Laura was here already, of course - I could see her as I was coming up the drive, still organising things. That girl is an absolute blessing to her mother, inspector. Anyway, Mr. Cope and his cousin arrived just after I did."

"Did you notice whether Mr. Cope seemed nervous or upset in any way?" interrupted Constable.

"Oh, quite the reverse, inspector. He was quite bubbling over with good humour. He was full of smiles and winks, almost as if he was enjoying some huge private joke. I remember, he made a sort of announcement of how perfect everyone looked sitting there, but to me, it all sounded a little false."

"Can you remember exactly what he said, sir?" enquired Copper.

Ivor Pugh frowned in recollection. "Not really, sergeant. It was all about Laura being so pretty, and her mother being the perfect lady, and how useful Albert was, and something about Helen's books, and then he made some rather acid remarks about Robin and Seymour, but of course they weren't there to hear them, so I suppose he felt free to let the cloven hoof show through a little. Oh heavens, what on earth am I saying?" He turned to Andy Constable. "Do please disregard that, inspector. That was quite unforgivable."

"De mortuis nil nisi bonum, vicar, is that it?" quoted Constable to Dave Copper's evident surprise. "I'm afraid in our line of work, speaking ill of the dead is sometimes the only way to reach the truth. So anyway, Mr. Cope made these remarks ...?"

"For which I couldn't see any particular point, inspector, except that they served to make everyone feel a little uncomfortable. It was rather like a bad stage performance. Anyway, Mr. Cope went out to his tent very soon after that, and Albert went out after him a few minutes later. But I can't tell you much about anyone else, because I had to pop out to see Brown Owl. The Brownies, sergeant," he added in response to Dave Copper's quizzical look. "And by the time I came back into the drawing room, Robin Allday and Seymour Cummings were there with the others. And then it was coming up to one o'clock, and Laura said she had forgotten to unlock the gate for people to come through and see Mr. Cope, and Sandra asked me if I would do it, so of course I said yes."

"So it was Lady Lawdown who sent you out to the Secret Garden?" enquired Constable. "Any particular reason, did she say?"

"Oh, only to save Laura the bother, inspector," replied the vicar hastily. "I really don't think you should read anything into it. Besides, she particularly asked me to pop in to see Mr. Cope to make sure that he was all ready."

Andy Constable smiled ruefully. "Sorry, reverend. You'll have to forgive my suspicious nature. I'm afraid it's part of the job. So what happened when you went outside?"

Reverend Pugh took a tremulous breath. "I'd taken Lady Lawdown's key to the gate, so I was on my way to unlock it, and as I passed the tent I called out 'Are you all ready, Mr Cope?'. But he didn't answer. So I thought I'd better make sure he was there, because there wouldn't be much point in letting people in if he'd gone off somewhere, would there? So I put my head in through the flap of the tent, and there he was."

"So what did you do, sir?" put in Dave Copper.

"I really didn't know what to do, sergeant," answered the vicar. "I went a little closer, but I could see that it was clear that he was dead. I didn't touch anything, though," he added anxiously. "But there was obviously nothing I could do for the poor man, so my first thought was to get back to the others and tell them. If you can call it a thought. I think I may have been a little muddled by then. I'd probably had a little more whisky than I ought to have done." He smiled weakly and made a helpless gesture with his hands. "I'm sorry, inspector - I don't suppose that helps you at all, does it?"

"Every little helps, vicar," replied Constable. "It all builds up the picture. But there's one thing which I've noticed. Everyone else refers to the dead man as Horace. You call him Mr. Cope. I don't wish to be impertinent, but were you not on good terms with the gentleman?"

The vicar shifted evasively. "Please don't think that, inspector. It wasn't a personal feeling at all. I hope that I know my Christian duty - we are commanded to love all our flock. But no - I'm afraid that I couldn't approve of the way Mr. Cope earned his living."

Dave Copper looked up from his notebook. His eyebrows rose. "Really, sir? How do you mean, exactly?"

"I mean the supernatural, sergeant. I always said all this modern mania for meddling about with occult powers would come to no good. All these television programmes about vampires and the like, and people talking about alternative moralities, and all these so-called magic shops selling tarot cards and spells and ... what are they called ... dream-catchers. I don't believe in fortune-telling."

Dave Copper was taken aback at the vicar's sudden vehemence. "But this business that Mr. Cope was supposed to do at the fete today - surely that was just a bit of harmless fun, sir?"

Reverend Pugh looked highly sceptic. "Hmmm. You may think it harmless, sergeant, but there are some very malign forces at work in this village. Yes, you may well look surprised, but it all goes back to pagan times. I can tell you all about it if you like."

"But I thought ..." Dave Copper was puzzled.

"Not that I have a personal interest, of course," explained the vicar. "But in my sort of job, it pays to know your enemy, if you see what I mean."

"Quite so, sir," commented Andy Constable. "But you mentioned malign forces. So what sort of things would these be?"

"There's the Dammett Well, for instance."

"What, the village pub's a malign force?" grinned Dave Copper. "That's a bit over the top, isn't it, vicar?"

"No, sergeant," said the vicar with a touch of asperity. "Not the pub - that was named after the well. I mean the Well itself."

"Sorry, sir - I'm not with you."

Reverend Pugh took a deep breath. "The Dammett Well, sergeant, is a spring in the churchyard, just behind the Lady Chapel. I'm told it's prehistoric - it's believed to have been some sort of Druid fertility shrine."

"I imagine that would be something of an embarrassment to the Church, Reverend, having a pagan shrine on church premises," commented Andy Constable.

"Oh, not at all, inspector," replied the vicar. "Quite the reverse, in fact. The early Christians were always re-using pagan religious sites when they built their first churches, you know. It meant they came with a ready-made congregation. Of course, there's no activity of that kind going on these days - although sometimes when the local girls get married, they like to leave their bridal bouquets at the well after they've done the photographs in the churchyard."

"And they do that because ..." Dave Copper's pencil was poised.

The vicar grew slightly pink. "As I say, sergeant, it was a fertility shrine, so you must draw your own conclusions. I try not to think too hard about their reasons. Particularly as half of them seem to have their own children acting as attendants during the wedding." Reverend Pugh cleared his throat. "I'm afraid I'm rather old-fashioned in some ways - I really would prefer to have the weddings come before the christenings, but we all have to move with the times, I suppose. I'm grateful that the young people want to come to church at all."

"Ah, so none of the certainties of the good old days, then?"

"Oh, sergeant, you couldn't be more wrong," smiled the vicar. "There was nothing 'good' about the old days. We have accounts of witches and black masses in medieval times, and one poor woman was even hanged from the old yew tree in the churchyard." His face grew solemn. "Yes, I'm afraid there are some really quite nasty things tucked away in the church records. Which reminds me, you wanted to ask me about Mr. Cope, didn't you?"

"Now that's interesting, Mr. Pugh," said Andy Constable. "Why should mention of the church records put you in mind of Horace Cope?"

"Because, inspector, the records are actually what brought Horace into the church more often than not. Including yesterday, as a matter of fact."

"Oh yes, sir?" The inspector raised his eyebrows.

"Why - do you think it may be important?"

"That all depends on what he was doing, doesn't it, sir," replied the inspector evenly.

"Well, he said he'd come to spend some time at the Well - he called it 'communing with the spirits', which I don't believe for a moment. I think he said these things simply to annoy me and see what my reaction would be. As I say, inspector, he did not have a particularly pleasant character sometimes, although I would not wish to speak ill of him, God rest his soul. But then he wanted to look at the records - again - and as I couldn't very well stop him, I left him to it."

"You say 'again'. Did Mr. Cope come to the church often?"

"Oh goodness, yes," said the vicar. "He wasn't what you'd call a regular worshipper - in fact, I'm not sure that he was any sort of worshipper, but I tend to follow Queen Elizabeth in that respect."

Dave Copper looked up from his notebook, puzzled. "Sorry, sir? Where on earth does the Queen come into this?"

"The first Queen Elizabeth, sergeant," explained the vicar. And as Dave Copper continued to look utterly baffled, "At the time of the Anglican settlement. She commented that as long as people behaved outwardly as she wished, she would not make 'windows into men's souls'."

"Hmmm," muttered Copper. "A few windows into men's souls would make my job a lot easier."

"You were telling us about Horace in church, vicar," said Andy Constable in an effort to get the investigation back on track.

"Of course, inspector. Yes, well, Mr. Cope did seem to spend an awful lot of time going through old records and registers. 'Historical research', he called it, but I really can't see how some of the recent registers could possibly be relevant to that, so I suspect that some of it may not have been all that historical. Certainly I can't see any relevance to his foretelling the future, or whatever it was he was claiming. And of course, that other so-called clairvoyant Seymour Cummings spends a lot of time in the village, but I believe that's because he's a very old friend of Sandra's - sorry, I mean Lady Lawdown."

"And would you say that Mr. Cummings and Her Ladyship are ...?" Dave Copper tailed off delicately.

"Oh, goodness me, nothing like that, I'm sure," said the vicar hastily. "No, they're simply old friends, and he visits her a great deal. Now, where was I?"

"Horace in church, sir?" repeated Constable a little wearily.

"I do beg your pardon, inspector. I'm afraid I do have something of a tendency to get sidetracked. But yes, Horace and Seymour in church! That's the point!"

"And the point would be ...?"

"It was only a few days ago. Tuesday, would it be? I'd seen Mr. Cope coming up through the churchyard, and I know it's probably most un-Christian, but I really didn't want to get involved in a conversation with him, so I tucked myself away in Sunday School corner. There's always a little task I can be getting on with, and on that particular day it was the choir hymn-books. I dare say you'll be shocked, inspector, but I have quite a regular job going through the books and rubbing out the rude remarks the choirboys write in them. Sometimes I don't know whether I should be horrified at some of the words the boys know, or impressed at the breadth of the education they're receiving at the village school. And some of the drawings, too - quite surprisingly anatomically correct. I think perhaps I shall have to make my sermons a little shorter in future. I confess I can be a bit long-winded at times, and the boys probably get bored, and as we all know, the devil will always find work for idle hands."

"And you were mentioning Mr. Cope and Mr. Cummings ..."

"Yes! Mr. Cope was ... well, I'm really not sure what exactly he was doing, because I was trying to avoid being noticed, and suddenly the door crashed open, which made me jump out of my skin, and Seymour Cummings came in and strode up to Mr. Cope and said 'Why are you trying to cause trouble for me?'. And in an extremely belligerent tone. I don't think I've ever seen Seymour so hot under the collar, so he was obviously thoroughly upset."

"And what was Mr. Cope's reaction to this?"

"Well, inspector, he smiled blandly, and said to Seymour that he had absolutely no idea what he was talking about."

"Did Mr. Cummings explain?"

"Seymour said he knew perfectly well that Horace had been on to the editor of the Daily Stir - that's the newspaper Seymour writes for, inspector; I don't know if you knew that - accusing Seymour of getting all his predictions off the internet. It sounded to me very much as if Horace was accusing Seymour of being a fraud."

"And do you reckon he is, sir?" put in Dave Copper.

"I really wouldn't like to say what Mr. Cummings's real beliefs are, sergeant," replied the vicar a little primly. "Judge

94

not, that ye be not judged. That's what we are taught. But I don't think that was what had made Seymour so worked up."

"So what do you think it was, sir?"

"Well, sergeant, the Daily Stir is owned by that Canadian who also owns the television station, and of course it's supposed to be a great secret, but everybody knows that there's a new show being planned which Seymour and Horace both wanted to be on. But of course, they couldn't both do it, so they were great rivals."

"Deadly rivals, as you might say," murmured Dave Copper.

"So then Seymour said that he wasn't going to be the victim of a smear campaign to keep him off the new show," continued the vicar, "and if Horace thought that he was going to stand in his way, he'd soon find out he was wrong."

"So in fact," interposed Andy Constable, "it sounds very much as if Mr. Cummings was threatening Mr. Cope?"

"I'm afraid you'll have to draw your own conclusions, inspector," replied the vicar. "I can only tell you what I heard. But then Horace replied 'I don't think there's a damned thing you can do about it, dear boy', in the most patronising tones imaginable, which seemed to make Seymour's blood boil even more, and he just blurted out 'Balls!' and stormed out. Very unholy language."

"But there was no actual violence, sir? Nothing physical?" Dave Copper sounded disappointed.

"Certainly not, sergeant. I really can't imagine anything of that sort happening."

"Well, it has now, hasn't it, sir?" commented Copper bluntly.

"Oh dear." Reverend Pugh sounded troubled. "Inspector, you don't suppose ... oh dear. Perhaps I should have said something. You know - blessed are the peacemakers, and so forth. Oh dear."

"Now I really don't think you should feel responsible, Mr. Pugh," remarked Andy Constable in a reassuring tone. "We are talking about something that happened several days ago. Plenty of time for tempers to have cooled. So we shan't be jumping to any conclusions. Let's just stick to gathering as much information as we can. Have there been any other incidents involving Mr. Cope that might be helpful?"

"Well ..." The vicar hesitated. "Not really, no. Well, not actually an incident ... I'm beginning to sound like a gossip, and I can't see that it can possibly be important."

"Suppose you tell us about whatever it was, sir, and then we shall know, shan't we? When did this non-incident occur?"

"Oh, it was the same afternoon - I suppose it must have been about half an hour after Seymour left. I was out in the church porch giving my hassocks a good beating ..."

An explosive snort burst forth from Dave Copper. In response to the inspector's glare, he swiftly buried his face back in his notebook.

"It's not funny at all, sergeant," rebuked the vicar. "They do get so very dusty, and it's an extremely dirty job, but there's nobody else to do it."

"Be that as it may, sir ..." Andy Constable tried once again to steer Mr. Pugh back to his narrative.

"Yes, inspector. As I say, I was in the porch, and Mr. Cope was coming out of the church just as Lady Lawdown arrived for bell-ringing practice."

"Her Ladyship's one of your bell-ringers?"

"Oh yes, inspector. She's really a very enthusiastic campanologist. I suppose you wouldn't expect it from the Lady of the Manor, but we can always rely on her to give a good strong pull on Little Jim."

Both detectives gazed at the vicar in total bewilderment.

"Sorry, sir ... little who?" Dave Copper's pencil was poised over his notebook.

"I do beg your pardon, sergeant. It's just one of our little parish jokes," explained Reverend Pugh. "Her Ladyship always rings the largest of our bells, which is named for St. James the Less, so of course we all call it Little Jim. Or I should say, 'her'. Bells are female, you know. Most people probably aren't aware of that." He smiled brightly.

"So Lady Lawdown arrived at the church ...?" Andy Constable made yet another effort to bring the vicar back to the point.

"Yes, inspector. As a matter of fact, she was a little early, or I don't suppose she and Mr. Cope would have met at all. Anyway, as it was, she was coming in as he was going out, and she just nodded to him, and he said, 'Hello, Alex. Off to do your bit for the serfs and peasants? I've been having a lovely time this afternoon'."

"And what was her response to that?"

"She just said 'What?', just like that. Abrupt. Frankly, and I really don't like to sound as if I'm criticising, but I thought she was rather short with him, which isn't like her at all. I've always found her to be extremely gracious. Anyway, she tried to carry on past Mr. Cope, but then he actually took hold of her by the arm to stop her and said 'I've been going through the parish records again. Great fun.' I can't explain why, but I got the impression that he was almost ... well, taunting her."

"Taunting her? But why would he do that? I was under the impression that they were friends."

"That's as may be, inspector. I'm just telling you what I heard. So then she just said 'Really?', and then Mr. Cope said, 'It's all so very interesting. Almost as interesting as the Family Records Office at Kew - you know, all the old Somerset House Births, Marriages and Deaths. Fascinating what turns up there sometimes. And even better, what doesn't turn up. Well, must go. I'll talk to you soon.' And then off he went, looking smug. Although now I think of it, he looked smug most of the time."

"And how did Her Ladyship look?" asked Constable.

"Ah, now that I'm afraid I can't tell you, inspector, because I was watching Mr. Cope go off down the path, and by the time I turned back, Her Ladyship had gone into the church, so I never had a chance to speak to her. And then all my other bell-ringers arrived, so of course we all went up into the tower, and I forgot all about it."

Chapter 9

"So what next, guv?"

The two detectives stood on the steps at the front door of the Hall, gazing out over the grounds towards the lake. Andy Constable seemed pre-occupied.

"Thinking time, sergeant. I'm going for a stroll."

"Do you want me to come with you, sir? We could go through my notes."

"No. You go and sit yourself down somewhere and look through them. See if you can find any gaps in any of the information people have given us. I swear someone's not telling us everything."

As he took the path which followed the reed-fringed shore of the lake, Inspector Constable cast his mind over the individuals in the case. It seemed a highly unlikely list of suspects, and yet each of them appeared to have a reason to dislike Horace Cope.

Lady Lawdown seemed the least likely person in the world to be a suspect in a murder case. The local aristocrat from the big house, a magistrate, on close terms with the Chief Constable of the county - all in all, a pillar of the community. Although, from one or two things which had been let drop, not a particularly wealthy one. Laura's comment that there was not much in the way of valuables in the house - the remarks about the roof - how many murders over the years had been committed for financial gain? And yet Horace's death seemed unlikely to benefit Lady Lawdown financially. Lady Lawdown's attitude seemed inconsistent - at one point, she was describing Horace Cope as a 'wretched little man', but in very nearly the same breath she was almost gushing in her praise for his talents as a clairvoyant. According to her daughter, Horace was a very old friend of the family, and yet the vicar was the unwilling witness to a confrontation between Lady Lawdown and Horace which seemed to have left him purring with self-satisfaction and her rattled and jumpy over something. But what? Had it anything to do with whatever Amelia Cook saw her bundling hurriedly into her handbag?

Lady Lawdown's daughter Laura was another whose relationship with Horace held inconsistencies. 'Uncle Horace', she called him. He gave her presents and took her out. In fact, he had been originally responsible in a way, having introduced her mother to Lord Lawdown, for Laura's position as a favoured daughter of a notable county family. Step-daughter, of course, as the child of Lady Lawdown's original marriage. So in the context of all this, what was the meaning of the conversation between Laura and Horace in Amelia Cook's teashop? Obviously it degenerated into unpleasantness, as Laura spoke of getting Horace stopped by using her mother's influence. And Horace's retort about Laura's mother not being much of a lady was hardly the remark of a good friend.

And then there was the other conversation in the 'Copper Kettle' which Amelia Cook had overheard. Andy Constable sent up a silent prayer of thanks for inquisitive and gossipy old ladies. If Horace Cope had been giving Helen Highwater's books bad reviews in his newspaper critic's column, it was hardly surprising that she in her turn should not be Horace's greatest fan. But Amelia had the impression that this was all water under the bridge, since Helen and Horace were having coffee together, but then some other factor seemed to have crept in. 'Don't you dare!', Helen had said. Dare what? Horace had talked about the value of something. With luck Amelia's memory would eventually come up with the missing remark which might throw more light on the exchange. But whatever it was, the meeting had not ended happily, that was clear. And Horace already had a copy of Helen's new book. But hadn't he turned down Helen's offer of a copy? Was he just threatening another bad review? Surely authors get used to such things. And a writer of Helen Highwater's standing, with the immense success of the Carrie Otter books, could afford to shrug off one unfavourable newspaper article.

Thinking about newspapers, Seymour Cummings had described himself as Horace Cope's deadly rival. Of course, he had been speaking in jest. But how funny did he actually find it? Not very funny at all, if the conversation which the vicar had overheard in the church was anything to go by. In fact, Horace seemed to be posing a considerable threat to Seymour's career. The only stock-in-trade which a professional clairvoyant has is his reputation, and if that is destroyed, he has nothing. The evidence of the email on Horace's computer showed that he was determined to put the largest of spokes into Seymour's wheel. If it became public knowledge that Seymour's predictions were not the result of his own psychic talents, but were plagiarised from other sources, whether the allegation were true or not, Seymour's career would be wrecked. Not only would his newspaper column be discredited, but any chance of the lucrative contract for the much-heralded television show would vanish. Seymour would find it virtually impossible to demonstrate his innocence - how do you prove a negative? He would be ruined. So Seymour's threat to Horace Cope may not have been an idle one, but the reaction of a desperate man.

As his eye fell on Gideon Porter, loading the last of his beer barrels on to a truck with the assistance of two beefy red-faced youngsters who, from the marked resemblance even at this distance, could only be his sons, Andy Constable was reminded of the conversations which the landlord had overheard at the Dammett Well Inn. What was it Gideon had said? 'You ever want to know anything, you just come and stand in my pub for a bit.' Certainly local knowledge helped. And local knowledge was an essential part of the work of a local solicitor, and without doubt, Robin Allday was another pillar of the Dammett Worthy community. In the course of his activities, a solicitor becomes privy to a great many confidences and secrets, and people need to trust such a man. Knowledge, it is said, is power. But the question was, not what Robin Allday knew about other people, but what Horace Cope knew about him. Horace evidently trusted Robin enough to draw up his will, but the mention of property dealings hung in the air in an uncomfortable fashion. There was evidently something Horace knew which rattled Robin badly, and it had to do with his handling of property transactions. Allegations of fraud hovered unspoken. But what was it that Horace knew, how did he come to know it, and most importantly of all, what was he proposing to do about it?

And then, last of all, Albert Ross. Horace's cousin, his closest - indeed, his only - relative, but for all that, an outsider in terms of the close-knit community of friends and family which made up Dammett Worthy. Horace's relationship with

Albert seemed to have been a strange mixture - on the one hand, Horace had taken him in when Albert had fallen on hard times, something for which Albert had shown a faintly pathetic gratitude - a rock, he had called Horace, a very generous man - but on the other, Horace had not exactly lavished an overdose of caring family consideration on his cousin. He housed him in the meanest accommodation compared with the overstated opulence of his own room. He used him almost as an unpaid servant, and ordered him about in front of others in a fashion verging on the humiliating. And again, the exchange overheard by Gideon showed that Horace was holding some kind of threat over Albert. Was the threat a result of Albert's suspected dishonesty, or had Albert tried to take some kind of compensation for himself as a payback for Horace's unpleasant treatment of him? And had the payback finally taken one step too far? Albert had been markedly jumpy during his interview with the police officers. Was this simply the natural nervousness of any person in that situation, or was it a result of the shock of the murder of his only family, or was it fear and guilt on account of his actions? As Constable knew only too well, sometimes the meekest worm will turn.

Everything came back to the character of Horace Cope. How often had he heard in his time as a junior detective that the key to the crime was so often to be found in the nature of the victim. So what sort of man was Horace Cope?

A creep. Andy Constable couldn't stop the words springing into his mind. On the surface, wealthy, cultured, well-respected. Influential, moving in high circles. A celebrity (how he hated that word!), appearing in the newspapers and on television. But as a person, not immediately likeable. Constable made a strenuous effort to put his personal thoughts aside, but he couldn't help shuddering at the lifestyle demonstrated by the furnishings with which Horace surrounded himself in his home. And the evidence of the various witnesses showed that Horace had a mercurial and unpredictable personality, at one moment charming and generous on the surface, but changing in moments to an air of syrupy menace or, on occasion, waspish malevolence. A collector of information, and a user of that information to his own benefit. In short, a blackmailer. But did he actually use the information, or did he simply hold it over the heads of his - was 'victims' too strong a word? - and to what end? There wasn't any evidence that Horace had derived any financial gains from his knowledge. So did he simply enjoy knowing what he knew, letting it be known that he had power over others, merely as an end in itself? It seemed so. Constable snorted. So, not only a creep, but a twisted creep. Sometimes, Andy Constable thought to himself, my job's not easy. He felt slightly depressed, a mood not helped by the fact that heavier curtains of drizzle had begun to drift in across the lake. He headed for the solitary cedar which towered over the front lawn half-way between the lake shore and the house, and hunched on the rustic wooden bench sheltering beneath it.

"Sir!"

Andy Constable looked up to see Dave Copper trotting across the lawn towards him, in his hand a plastic bag. Copper seated himself alongside the inspector, puffing slightly.

"I reckon you may be interested in this, sir. Just found it in the library, crumpled up in the waste-paper basket."

"What were you doing ferreting about in the waste-paper basket?"

"Dropped my notebook, sir. Fished it out, found this underneath it."

"So what is it?"

"Letter to Robin Allday, sir. Dated the day before yesterday. Listen to this."

The bag was the usual clear seal-able type used to contain items of evidence. Inside, crumpled but smoothed out so that it could be read, was a letter on Law Society headed notepaper, addressed to Robin Allday at his chambers in Dammett Worthy High Street.

"'Dear Mr. Allday, As a result of certain information which has come into our possession, we should be grateful if you would attend a preliminary hearing at these premises on Wednesday of next week. We apologise for the short notice given to you, but we believe that the gravity of the allegations required urgent action. You may bring an additional legal advisor should you think it appropriate'."

"Who's it from?"

"Some woman called Julie Noated, sir. Secretary of the Disciplinary Board, it says. So what do you reckon that's all about?"

Andy Constable raised an eyebrow. "We know exactly what it's about, sergeant. In fact, I've just been thinking about Mr. Allday and what we've been told about some of his activities. Maybe a bit of fiddling taxes, maybe a bit of property fraud. And it looks very much as if somebody has blown the gaff on Mr. Allday to his professional authorities."

"That somebody being Horace Cope, sir?"

"Who else, sergeant? We can check very easily - you can give them a call on Monday."

Dave Copper grinned broadly. "Well then, we've got him, haven't we, sir? Perfect motive. Horace threatens Robin, Robin won't play ball, so Horace spills the beans and Robin bops him one. End of. Let's go get him."

"Hold your horses, Copper," smiled Constable, amused at his colleague's eagerness. "There are still some things that don't quite fit." He began to pace up and down. "For a start, until we know exactly what this 'certain information' is, we can't be at all sure that Horace Cope had anything to do with providing it."

"No, sir," put in Copper, "but it'd be just like him, from everything people have told us, wouldn't it?"

"That I grant you, sergeant, but we shan't know for certain until Monday. And in any case, we've heard a lot about Horace Cope making all these meaningful remarks to everybody, but we haven't got any evidence as yet that he actually did anything about any of them. I think our Mr. Cope was the sort of man who enjoyed having power over people because of what he knew about them. But once you actually use the threat, it's gone. You can't use it again. And if Horace Cope had actually gone ahead and revealed what he knew about Robin Allday, what would be the point of Robin killing him? The cat's already out of the bag."

"Maybe he killed him to protect somebody else, sir."

Andy Constable paused. "That, Sergeant Copper, is a remarkably astute observation. Well done. And you would have in mind ...?"

"Well, sir, Miss Biding is a very attractive young lady. And she does fit in with this property thing somewhere."

"Excellent thinking, Copper. I like it. And that could perhaps account for one thing which is puzzling me, which you

103

don't seem to have thought of."

"What's that, sir?" asked Copper.

"The letter itself," explained Constable, taking it from his colleague's hand and examining it. "What on earth is it doing in the library at Dammett Hall when it's addressed to Robin Allday's office? Unless he brought it up here to show to ..."

"Laura Biding!" exclaimed the two policemen in unison.

"Because she was threatened by Horace Cope as well, and Robin's got a soft spot for her. And that could be why he would have killed Horace Cope."

"Or," interrupted Copper, "Laura's also got a soft spot for Robin, so she killed Horace so as to try and protect Robin!"

"And now you're starting to give me a headache," said Constable. "If we start getting into motives where people are killing people to protect other people, there'll never be an end to it. We shall have Lady Lawdown protecting her daughter, and Helen Highwater protecting Lady Lawdown, and Seymour Cummings protecting goodness-knows-who, and the vicar killing Horace Cope off for the greater good of his parishioners! Let's stick to what we know at the moment, and what we know is that we don't know what this letter tells us."

"No, sir." Dave Copper shook himself slightly. "I mean, yes, sir. So do you want me to go and find out?"

"We'll both go, sergeant. I think we've done enough speculating for the moment. I think it's time we went and had another little chat with our suspects. They've had plenty of time to sit and wonder what's going on - I'm sure they'll be starting to get a bit twitchy now, so we may get a bit more of the truth out of them. It's worth a try. I still can't rule any of them out at the moment, and the more I find out about Horace Cope, the more surprised I am that somebody didn't murder him long ago."

Dave Copper grimaced. "He really was quite a nasty piece of work, Mr. Cope, wasn't he, sir?"

Andy Constable nodded. "I rather think you're right, sergeant. But now he's a murdered nasty piece of work, which means we have our job to do. And I don't know about you, but I'm getting cold and wet. Come on."

Chapter 10

At the front door of Dammett Hall, the village policeman was maintaining his vigil, although by now he was starting to droop a little. Andy Constable felt sorry for him.

"How are we, Collins? Anything to report?"

"Not really, sir. Gideon Porter's gone back down to the pub, but he said he had your okay for that. And I think most of the other stall-holders have gone off as well, so there's hardly anybody around now. Except for in the house, that is."

"And are all our suspects still safely tucked up where we left them?"

Collins grinned. "Far as I know, sir. I haven't heard a peep out of them. Oh, except for that Miss Cook, sir. She wanted to know how long you wanted her to stay here - something about getting the scones done for this afternoon's cream teas, and whether she ought to do them up here or down at her tearooms. She was all in a bit of a flap, sir, but then she usually is, to be honest, but I calmed her down."

"Well done, Collins." Andy Constable looked at the steadily increasing rain advancing towards the house. "Look, there's no point in you standing here freezing to death and getting wet. Go and see Miss Cook and tell her we'll have a chat with her later. We can go down to the village if need be. And with a bit of luck, she might let you have a cup of tea."

"And tell her you can have that bit of cake she promised me," put in Dave Copper with a smile.

"Right you are, sir. Thank you." And a relieved-looking Collins headed in the direction of the kitchen.

Seven weary faces turned to see the two detectives as they entered the library, where an awkward silence seemed to be reigning. The Reverend Pugh, who had regained a considerably more normal colour than had been the case during his conversation with the officers, rose at once and came towards Inspector Constable.

"Inspector, might I have a word?"

"By all means, Mr. Pugh. What can I do for you?"

"I was wondering how much longer you wanted me to

105

stay," explained the vicar anxiously. "Of course, I'm only too happy to do my duty, and if you need me here any longer I'm quite prepared to remain as long as I can be useful, but I honestly don't know that I can tell you any more than I've already said, and what is beginning to trouble me is that I may not be back to St. Salyve's in time to prepare properly for this evening's service, and I really do think that there is likely to be a number of my flock who are going to be disturbed by today's events, so of course they will be looking to the church for guidance and comfort, and I feel that I need a time of quiet and calm to prepare some remarks for them in my sermon, which of course under the present circumstances I might find ... er ... somewhat difficult ..." He glanced meaningfully at the others in the room. "So if it's no trouble, and you really think you can spare me, I would be so terribly grateful ..."

"Please, Mr. Pugh, don't give it another thought," said the inspector, stopping the vicar's flow with some difficulty. "I'm sure if there's anything else we need to speak to you about, we shall be able to find you quite easily."

At that moment, there came a tap at the library door, and P.C. Collins put his head into the room.

"Sorry to interrupt you, sir, but it's Miss Cook. She says can you pop in and see her, because she's remembered what it is she forgot, and it was the batch of scones that did it, and it wasn't mother at all. I have no idea what she's on about, but she seemed quite excited. And she'd like to get on, if you don't mind, sir."

"Thank you, Collins. Tell her we'll be with her as soon as we can. And then can you run Mr. Pugh back down to the village, please. Can't have him getting wet in this rain."

"Will do, sir." Collins disappeared back into the hall.

"That's really extremely good of you, inspector," said the vicar. "But I wouldn't want to put that young man to any trouble, and I'm perfectly happy to walk, even though it does look rather damp out there ..."

"Not at all, Mr. Pugh." said Constable, briskly. "Copper ...?" And at a nod from the inspector, the sergeant ushered the still-expostulating clergyman out into the hall. Constable turned back to the remaining six people in the room, who regarded him with a mixture of expectation and apprehension.

106

"I am very sorry to have kept you all for what must seem like a very long time, ladies and gentlemen." Andy Constable was at his most emollient. "I'm afraid these matters are not always quick and easy to resolve. But I have hopes that we may not need to detain you for very much longer."

"I sincerely hope not, inspector," said Lady Lawdown sharply, rising to her feet. "It is not at all pleasant to be cooped up almost like a prisoner in one's own house, and I'm not at all sure that such a thing is entirely within your rules of conduct. Indeed, I shall definitely consider having a serious word with the Chief Constable next time we meet, which I'm sure will be very soon." She glared at the detective.

Andy Constable smiled calmly. "I assure you, my lady, that we are doing everything we possibly can as quickly as we can. And of course, nobody could be happier than me if you wish to discuss the matter with the Chief, because I'm sure he would be delighted to explain the exact procedures we follow so that there will be no doubt in your mind for future reference." He looked levelly at Lady Lawdown, whose eyes wavered and then fell.

"But as it happens," he continued, "we wanted to have a further word with everyone here, and perhaps it would be a good idea to start with your ladyship. After all, the sooner we begin ... Perhaps we might use the library again, if that would be convenient."

"Oh. Very well, inspector. If that is what you wish."

"After you, my lady." He turned to the others. "If you wouldn't mind waiting here for a little longer ..." Murmurs of weary agreement followed him out of the room.

"On my way, sir." A breathless Collins emerged through the green baize door to the kitchen corridor. He almost scampered in the direction of the front door where Sergeant Copper stood patiently listening to a still-gesticulating vicar, then turned back. "Oh, by the way, sir. Miss Cook. She says she's a bit pushed, so she's made a note ..."

"Yes, yes, thank you, Collins," interrupted the inspector. "We'll get to her as soon as we can. You just carry on." He held the library door open for Lady Lawdown, and the two detectives followed her into the room as Collins led the vicar out through the front door.

Constable took his place behind the desk again as Copper seated himself discreetly to one side. Lady Lawdown poised herself elegantly on the edge of a leather tub chair and looked at the inspector with eyebrows raised.

"Well?"

Constable declined to be intimidated. "Well, my lady, there are a few things we'd like to verify about the sequence of events this afternoon, so I'm sure you'll be able to assist us with that."

"Very well, inspector, although I really don't see how any of us could possibly have had the chance to murder Horace."

"And yet," remarked Constable drily, "somebody did. And what I need to know is who was where and when, so that I can decide who did have that chance."

Lady Lawdown sighed. "As I'm sure you already know, inspector, we were all together in the drawing room having drinks from twelve o'clock."

"We? And that would be exactly ...?"

"Well, everybody ... Laura and myself, Helen, Seymour, the vicar of course, Horace and Albert, and Robin. Oh no, just a minute ... Robin and Seymour weren't there at twelve, because they didn't come in until later. I'd forgotten that."

"So what about Mr. Cope's exact movements?" asked Constable. "Can you remember those?"

"Oh, that's perfectly simple, inspector. Sorry, I thought you already knew. Horace and Albert arrived at twelve o'clock - no, in fact it was more like five past, because the vicar had got here at twelve exactly. I know that, because I remember the hall clock was striking as Helen went out to fetch him in. So Horace was actually a few minutes late, but I don't suppose that really matters, does it, because after all he was still alive then. Oh, and he brought me some beautiful flowers ..." She broke off. "That reminds me, I must put them in water. I'm sure they're still sitting on the piano, so if I don't do something about them they'll be as dead as ... well, as dead as Horace!" She gave a slightly hysterical laugh. "I do apologise, inspector. That was in extremely poor taste, but this is all becoming a little too much for me."

"Quite so, your ladyship. But if we can stick to what

108

actually happened ..."

"Ah. Yes. Well, Horace had a quick drink, which I poured for him - oh dear, inspector, I hope you don't think that I - oh no, of course, silly of me, he wasn't poisoned, was he?"

"No, my lady," replied Constable, bluntly. "It was a great deal bloodier than that."

"Please, inspector. I can hardly bear to think of it." Lady Lawdown shuddered, took a deep breath and seemed to pull herself together. "So, Horace finished his drink quite quickly, because he said he had better go off and get things ready, and he wanted Albert to go with him at that point, but it was Laura I think who stopped Albert, so Horace stumped off rather grumpily on his own. So that would have been - oh, it must have been somewhere between five and ten past twelve. It was all very quick."

"Was there some reason for not wanting Albert to go with Mr. Cope?" enquired the inspector.

"Not at all, not really," replied Lady Lawdown. "It's just that - poor Albert, he's always at Horace's beck and call, and Horace always seems to be barking orders at him, so I think we all feel a little sorry for him. Albert, that is. It was just to give the poor little man a few moments respite. But to be honest, it didn't really do much good - Albert seemed most ill-at-ease, and looked as if he really didn't want to be there at all, so he almost gulped down his drink and said he ought to go and help Horace, so off he went. And I suppose that must have been ten past or so."

"And was he gone long?"

"Oh, hardly any time at all. Minutes." She wrinkled her brow in thought. "Actually, he was gone until Laura came back, so that must have been about twenty minutes altogether. Isn't it funny how you don't notice the time slip past?"

Dave Copper looked up. "Sorry to interrupt, sir, but did her ladyship say that Miss Biding also left the drawing room?"

Lady Lawdown turned to the sergeant. "Oh yes, but only for a moment to fetch some drinks." She smiled. "I expect I shouldn't tell you this, but the vicar had seen off more than his fair share of the whisky. I dare say it was to steady his nerves, but I think it may have been that as much as the shock of finding Horace which made him keel over."

"And did Miss Biding leave the drawing room again after she returned?" asked Copper.

"Not for a moment," stated Lady Lawdown firmly. "She was going to, because she had forgotten to unlock the gate to the Secret Garden, but I asked Mr. Pugh to do it ... Oh dear!"

"Yes, my lady? What is it?"

"I've just thought. Really, it's my fault that Mr. Pugh had that terrible shock. Poor man. But if he hadn't gone, then it would have been Laura who discovered Horace's body. Oh, how awful."

"Indeed," said Constable. "Well, I think that's all we need from your ladyship for the moment." Lady Lawdown rose to leave. "Oh, just one thing before you go, my lady. Would you have any knowledge of a small ad placed in the name of 'L'?"

Lady Lawdown gazed at the inspector. "A small ad, inspector? What on earth do you mean?"

"Just a small advertisement in the classified columns of a newspaper, my lady. I'm afraid we don't know which paper."

"But what sort of advertisement? Was it Births, Marriages and Deaths, or what?"

Constable smiled slightly. "Oh no, my lady, nothing like that. It was just something in the Personal Services column."

"Personal Services? I'm sorry, inspector, but I really can't help you," replied Lady Lawdown frostily. "I don't believe I've ever read the Personal Services column. From what little I've heard, I can't think that there would be anything in it to interest me. So if you have quite finished with me ...?"

"Only one more question if I may, my lady. You mention the Births, Marriages and Deaths. Do you have a special fascination for these things?"

Lady Lawdown seemed taken aback by the enquiry. "What an odd question, inspector. Why should I?"

"So the local church records and documents would not be of specific interest to you?"

"No, not especially. Why do you ask?"

"So if somebody said they had seen you with some papers in the church ...?" Constable raised his eyebrows and waited.

"Then they would be mistaken, inspector," said Lady Lawdown, firmly. "So, if you have no other questions, I'm sure you will be wanting to speak to the others. Is there anyone in particular that you would like to see first?"

Constable thought for a moment. "Perhaps if you would ask Mr. Ross if he would be good enough to join us. And may I just thank your ladyship for your help. It's been most useful."

Lady Lawdown appeared to be about to reply, but then simply inclined her head graciously, poise seemingly restored, and left the room.

Andy Constable thumped the desk in frustration. "Damn it, Copper, why can't people tell us the truth?"

"There's certainly something she's not telling us, sir. But what was all this Births, Marriages and Deaths business all about? What's that got to do with anything?"

"Perhaps it's got something to do with the letter from the Family Records office. I think we need to have a closer look at that."

A timid tap was heard at the library door. The two detectives looked at one another.

"Albert Ross!" they said in unison. Dave Copper went to the door and ushered Albert into the room.

"Lady Lawdown said you wanted to see me, inspector. I honestly don't know that I can add any more to what I said before. I've told you everything I know."

"Ah, but that's not strictly true, is it, Mr. Ross," said Constable. "I think there are quite a few things you haven't told us. For instance, you said to us that you went out to help your cousin get ready for the fete, and to do his make-up for his character as the fortune-teller."

Albert licked his lips. "That's right - I did. It was the eyes, you see. He couldn't see to do them properly without his glasses, you see, but of course he couldn't wear his glasses, so that's why he needed me."

"Yes, Mr. Ross, I quite understand," replied Constable. "There's just one problem. Mr. Cope wasn't actually wearing any eye make-up when he was found. So although you may have gone out to his tent with the intention of helping him to prepare, when you got there you didn't actually do it. So what did you do?"

Albert Ross gaped at the inspector. "Oh dear." Tears came to his eyes. "I really didn't do it, inspector. How could I?

What reason would I have?"

Constable was unmoved. "Well, Mr. Ross, from what we can gather, quite a few reasons. Let's start with just one - the fact that you were about to lose your home."

"How did you know about that?" asked Albert in astonishment.

"You would be amazed at the things we know, Mr. Ross," replied Constable. "So why don't you tell us about it."

Albert seemed to deflate as he slumped further into his chair. "All right, inspector. I'll tell you. I didn't go to help Horace set his things up - well, I did, but I wanted something else as well. I wanted one last chance to persuade him to change his mind about throwing me out of the cottage."

"And why was he intending to throw you out, Mr. Ross?"

Albert shifted in his seat. "Well, inspector ... it was all rather personal. I'd really rather not go into it." He blinked. "Er ... family reasons."

"Family reasons, eh?" Constable's tone was dry. "Which some people might think odd, since you two were the only family you had. That is right, isn't it, Mr. Ross?"

"Yes."

"So there's another reason which some might think gave you a motive to kill your cousin, sir. They might assume that you would have expectations of inheriting his money, mightn't they? And it looks as if that might be quite a tidy sum, which from what you told us about your financial situation, would be very useful to you. Wouldn't it?"

Albert Ross refused to meet the inspector's eye, and remained looking at his hands which twisted awkwardly in his lap.

"So, Mr. Ross," persisted Constable, "you said you wanted to try to persuade Mr. Cope to change his mind. Did you succeed?"

"No, inspector, I didn't. I even begged him, but it wasn't any use. He wouldn't budge. And so I left."

"Just like that? You're all set to be thrown out on to the street, your cousin is refusing to help you, so you just turn and go? You do nothing?"

Albert smiled wanly. "What do you think I did, inspector? I'm not a violent man. Yes, I just turned and left. And

112

I swear that Horace was perfectly all right when I last saw him. In fact, he was better than all right. You never knew him, inspector. You don't know how smug he could be whenever he got his own way over people. So yes, he was perfectly all right. He had that smile he used to wear. So I left."

"And did what, Mr. Ross? Did you go straight back and join the others?" asked Dave Copper, pen poised over his notebook.

"I really didn't know what to do, sergeant," said Albert. "I was at the end of my tether, and I even thought of just going back to the cottage and packing up my few bits and pieces and just quietly going away somewhere. I've no idea where - I just wanted to get away. But then I had a thought, and I went upstairs to find Seymour."

"What made you want to see Mr. Cummings, sir?"

"I don't know. I just thought he might know of some way of putting pressure on Horace to make him change his mind. I suppose I hoped that he might know something about Horace - I thought if Horace knows all these things about other people, and Seymour and Horace have been rivals in the business all these years ..." He tailed off.

"So you thought you'd see if you could do a little reverse blackmail of your own, eh?" remarked Constable. "It seems to have been quite a family trait. So, any luck?"

"No, inspector. I just sat there in Seymour's room until he came back, and then I told him everything. He said he couldn't really think of anything offhand, but he'd try to help, not that he and Horace were exactly the best of friends. He seemed rather vague, but to be honest, I was just glad of someone to talk to, even though I don't think he was really listening properly. Anyway, after I'd finished, we just went back downstairs to the drawing room together."

"Would you know what time that was, sir?" enquired Copper.

"Yes, I do remember that, sergeant," said Albert. "It was exactly half-past twelve, because the clock at the foot of the stairs was striking just as we came down, and Laura was just coming back with a bottle of whisky, and Seymour made some remark about needing a drink, so we went into the drawing room to join the others. And that's where I stayed all the time.

113

You can ask anyone."

"We shall, Mr. Ross, don't you worry. But thank you for that. I think I've got it all noted down quite clearly."

"Oh. Er. Good." Albert hesitated. "Was ... was that all, then, inspector? Only I ...?"

"Yes, I think so, Mr. Ross." Inspector Constable's tone indicated that it probably wasn't. "We'll have a word with some of the others now. Perhaps if you could ask Miss Highwater if she would spare us a few minutes, that would be very kind." And as Albert rose to go, "Oh, and if you wouldn't mind just remaining in the drawing room for the time being - just in case we need another little chat." He smiled urbanely.

"I can't make him out at all, sir," remarked Dave Copper as the door closed behind Albert. "He seems such a feeble specimen, you can't really imagine him getting himself together for long enough to do anything to anyone."

Andy Constable gave a short laugh. "Come on, Copper - you know better than that. We've had enough cases where the worm turns. Plus, I think there's more to our Mr. Ross than meets the eye. What about this business about the vanishing antiques that Gideon Porter told us about? Gaps on the walls at Mr. Cope's cottage, gaps on the shelves - I shouldn't be a bit surprised if Mr. Porter had the rights of it, and it looks as if Mr. Ross was crafty enough to pull that off and dispose of the stuff without getting caught out by our local colleagues. So let's not put him quite out of the picture just yet. If Horace Cope was worth what it seems he was, what with the cottage and everything, that would be a better motive to kill him than a lot we've known."

Dave Copper glanced at his notebook. "And there's his movements, sir. Do the timings sound a bit iffy to you?"

"Just a bit, Copper."

At that moment, there was a firm knock at the door, and Helen Highwater strode briskly into the room. "You wished to see me, I believe." She seated herself opposite the inspector. "What can I do for you?"

"It's largely a question of confirming a few details about what people were doing and when, Miss Highwater," responded Constable smoothly. "Now there's one point that's just come up, while I think of it. Mr. Ross has just told us that he left the

114

drawing room to go to help his cousin prepare for the fete, and he returned at twelve thirty. Can you help us with that?"

"Ah, now as it happens, I can, inspector, and Albert is quite right. It was exactly half past because the hall clock was striking, and I saw them all go into the drawing room together. They were only just ahead of me."

"Sorry, madam ..." Constable was perplexed. "All?"

"Oh yes. Albert was just coming downstairs with Seymour, and Laura came out of this room at the same time."

"So Miss Biding was out of the drawing room as well?"

"Certainly, inspector. Sorry, didn't you know?"

"Actually, no, we didn't, madam." Inspector Constable's voice gave nothing away, and he raised his eyebrows in expectation. "So perhaps you'd be good enough to tell us."

"It's perfectly simple, inspector. Sandra had sent Laura off to get some more drinks, which I suppose would have been about twenty past twelve."

"And do you know where she went?"

"Of course. She went to the butler's pantry."

"Butler's pantry?" broke in Dave Copper. "Where exactly is that, madam? We weren't shown anything like that when Miss Biding explained the layout of the house to us."

"It's that little room under the staircase, sergeant," replied Helen. "I dare say they didn't think of it, because of course it isn't used as a butler's pantry these days. In fact, there hasn't been a butler for years - not since Peter died."

"Peter being who ... the last butler?"

"Oh goodness no, sergeant," laughed Helen. "Peter was Lord Lawdown - Sandra's husband. But of course, when he died there were all the death duties, so some things had to go. Do you know, there used to be a staff of fourteen in the house and gardens when I was a girl, but not any more. It would be lovely if Sandra could afford a butler, poor dear, but she's on her uppers." Her hand went to her mouth and she turned to Andy Constable. "Oh heavens - I do hope you won't repeat that, inspector. I really shouldn't have let it slip out. But that's one of the reasons that Sandra keeps the fete going these days - it's a very good way of raising money to help keep up the house."

"If we could just return to the point, madam," said Constable. "The butler's pantry ...?"

"I'm sorry, inspector. Yes, it's a room under the stairs, with the old strongroom for the silver and the cupboard for the wines. It's bigger than you'd think. There's the door from the hall, which you probably didn't notice because it's quite well hidden in the panelling, and there's the door through from the kitchen, but I think they keep that one locked all the time. So that's where Laura was going to get some drink - whisky, I think."

"And you say you saw the others go back into the drawing room all together, Miss Highwater. Which means, of course, that you also left the room."

"Oh, yes. Yes, I did. I said I'd go with Laura to give her a hand. But then as it was, she only wanted the one bottle of whisky, so she didn't really need me at all, but then she said she had to make a phone call from the library, so I said I'd pop out to the flower room to get a vase for the flowers Horace had brought Sandra."

Andy Constable leaned forward. "Now that is possibly quite interesting, Miss Highwater. Did Miss Biding mention who it was that she was going to call?"

"I'm sorry, inspector, she didn't," replied Helen. "She was a little bit awkward about it, so I didn't like to ask."

"Well, no matter, madam," said Constable breezily. "We shall just have to ask her, shan't we? So then ...?"

"Well, then we all went back into the drawing room to join Sandra. I think we all stayed there until the vicar came back, and you know what happened after that."

"Indeed we do, Miss Highwater, so we needn't go into that again. But I do have one or two things I'd just like to clarify. Firstly, the matter of your new book. When we visited Mr. Cope's cottage, we found a copy of the new Carrie Otter book in Mr. Cope's study. But from what I gather, it isn't available yet. So how do you suppose that came about?"

Helen laughed. "Gracious, inspector, there's no mystery about that at all. Horace was a book critic - I'd let him have a copy in advance for his review column. It's quite normal in publishing, you know."

"I see," said Constable. "Now I had the impression that Mr. Cope turned down your offer as unnecessary, from something Miss Cook said she heard."

"Oh inspector, I shouldn't pay too much attention to what Amelia says," replied Helen. "She's always far too busy running about making scones and suchlike to know what goes on. Well, you've talked to her - she's a dear soul, but you know what she's like."

Constable smiled understandingly. "We do, Miss Highwater. Well, I think that will do for now, so I won't keep you any longer. But if you could ask Mr. Cummings to pop through, that would be very kind."

"Of course, inspector." Helen rose and moved to the door.

Constable turned to his colleague. "Copper, don't let me forget to have another word with Miss Cook when we've finished with Mr. Cummings and the others."

Helen turned, her hand on the doorknob. "Oh, I say ..."

"Yes, Miss Highwater. What is it?"

"I've just realised, inspector. If Seymour and the rest of us went into the drawing room at half past twelve, that would mean that Sandra had been on her own while we were out of the room. She could have done anything - I hadn't thought of that." She closed the door quietly behind her.

Chapter 11

"I'm afraid I have something of a confession to make, inspector. I haven't been completely straight with you."

Seymour Cummings took his seat in front of the library desk with an air of a schoolboy summoned to the headmaster's study to account for his misdeeds. Beneath his tan, he looked pale.

Andy Constable gave a faint smile. "To be frank, Mr. Cummings, in my experience, hardly anybody is ever completely straight with us during an investigation, particularly when it's a question of murder. But I have to say that it's a refreshing change to have a suspect actually volunteer the information."

"A suspect? So you think that I might have ...?"

"Suspect purely in a technical sense, Mr. Cummings," explained Constable in soothing tones. "As someone who was present at the scene of the crime, you fall into the same category as everyone else in the house. Perhaps I should have said 'person under investigation'. Or 'person helping us with our enquiries'. Does that help?"

Seymour still looked anxious. "In all honesty, inspector, I think it makes it sound worse," he said ruefully. "And Helen says you were asking about my movements this morning, and I suddenly realised that I thought I had an alibi, but I haven't. Mind you, don't they say that the people with the strongest alibis are usually the chief suspects?" He gazed hopefully at the two detectives.

"Suppose you just tell us what it is you haven't been completely straight about, Mr. Cummings, and we'll take it from there."

"Of course, inspector."

"Shall we take it from mid-day today, sir, when I understand Lady Lawdown's little party was due to begin and Mr. Cope arrived on the premises."

"Ah, well that's the thing, inspector. I should have been in the drawing room at twelve for this little drinks thing of Sandra's, but I didn't really fancy having to be nice to Horace, so

I went for a bit of a walk round the grounds to kill time. I needed to think."

Andy Constable exchanged a glance with Dave Copper. "And would you like to tell us what it was you needed to think about, sir?"

Seymour sighed. "It's this blasted television show - you remember, 'Seeing Stars'. I'd thought it was all cut and dried that Horace was going to get the presenter's job, which didn't really worry me overmuch, because I've got plenty of other irons in the fire. But then somebody, and I can't remember who it was, said that my name had also come up as a possibility, so I started to get quite excited about that. That was when it started."

"Sorry, sir. When what started?"

"Horace's campaign." Seymour frowned. "Yes, I suppose you would have to call it that. Oh, we've never been friends - we would meet socially and be superficially polite, but that was as far as it went. But then word got around that he was dripping poison into the ears of anyone who would listen about me, and generally trying to put a spoke in."

"In any particular way, sir?" asked Constable blandly, eyebrows raised.

Seymour blushed. "Well ... um ... not that I can think of specifically, inspector."

"Would it help, sir, if I mentioned that we've seen an email to Mr. Cope from your editor?"

"To Horace from Kelvin? What on earth is Kelvin Hastings doing sending emails to Horace?"

"It was actually a reply, sir," explained Constable. "But I think that that shouldn't come as a surprise to you, should it, sir? I think you knew that Mr. Cope had been in touch with your newspaper, and I think that you weren't too pleased about it, were you? From what we've been told, that is."

"Well, I don't know who's told you that, inspector," blustered Seymour. "I know Horace used to derive a lot of pleasure from little bits of gossip, but you really mustn't believe everything you hear."

Constable sighed patiently. "Mr. Cummings, we shall get on a great deal better if we stick to the truth. You did say that you were going to be straight with us, so I'll be straight with you. We know very well that you had a row in the church the other day with Mr. Cope. We know very well that you knew all about his approach to your editor regarding the allegation that your work was - well, shall we say, not all your own work. We know very well that in fact you virtually threatened Mr. Cope. And the reason we know all this is that your conversation was overheard by Mr. Pugh, who was in the church at the time."

Seymour crumpled. "I see. Well, if you know all that, inspector, there isn't really a lot of point in my denying it, is there?" He thumped his fist on his knee. "Blast!" He looked up at the detective and seemed to be searching for words. "Inspector ... just how widely known is this? I mean, the vicar's told you, and if my editor's had Horace on to him with all the gory details ..."

"I think you can rely on Mr. Pugh not to go spreading talk, Mr. Cummings," replied Constable. "And as for your editor, from the tone of the reply, it looks as if Mr. Cope's approach to him was couched in fairly oblique terms, and in fact, from what I can recall, your editor speaks of you quite confidently. So perhaps Mr. Cope was saving the gory details, as you put it, for the meeting itself."

"What meeting?" Seymour sounded surprised. "I don't know anything about a meeting."

"Do you not, sir?" Andy Constable was carefully neutral. "It seems that Mr. Cope was due to have a meeting with Mr. Hastings next week."

"And that's probably when he would have ... oh hell." A thought seemed to strike Seymour and he looked suddenly hopeful. "So that means that nobody's actually said anything yet?"

"It seems not, sir."

"Well, thank heavens for that, at any rate. It's not as bad as it could have been. I'm sorry, inspector - you'll think I sound heartless," explained Seymour, "but it's all a matter of reputation, you see. What's that bit in 'Othello' about 'he who steals my good name', or something like that? In my business, it's really all a matter of reputation, and it's not easy to get that back if somebody's threatening to destroy it."

"Which Mr. Cope was about to do, it seems. Now there's a motive. So the timing of his death is a bit of luck for you, in a way, sir. Not, of course, wishing to sound heartless."

"No." Seymour seemed lost for words.

"So, on the question of timing," continued Constable, "let's get back to your own movements. Sergeant, I think you've got some notes on that?"

"Yes, sir." Dave Copper thumbed back through his notebook. "You told us you went out for a walk in the grounds before twelve, so you didn't see Mr. Cope when he arrived. The next thing we know is that you returned to the drawing room at half past twelve. So can you tell us where you were during that time?"

Seymour sighed helplessly. "Actually, sergeant, I probably can't in any detail. I don't suppose that does me any good at all, does it?"

"Then let's just do it bit by bit, sir. You left the house ..."

"Yes. I took the key from the flower room and went out through the gate in the Secret Garden because I didn't want to run into anyone arriving through the front door."

Dave Copper turned to his superior. "In which case, sir, that means that the gate was left open while Mr. Cope was setting up. That's not going to help us, is it?"

"No, sergeant, it wasn't," said Seymour hastily. "I locked it behind me. It's never left open. Sandra's got us all well trained, ever since they had that break-in."

"I see, sir. So, what next? You went for a walk ...?"

"Yes. I can't tell you exactly where, because I wasn't paying too much attention - somewhere up through the woods at the back of the house, I think, because everybody was getting things ready for the fete at the front of the house, and I wasn't really in the mood for mixing with people. But I do know I looked at my watch and I thought that I ought to get back indoors and do my bit for Sandra, so then I came back in through the kitchen. I think that must have been getting on for twenty-five past twelve."

"Can anyone vouch for that, sir?"

"Amelia. She had to unlock the kitchen door to let me in. Sandra's rules again, but I suppose that's quite a useful thing this time. You know, alibi and so on."

"Assuming you need one, of course, sir," remarked Copper, smiling blandly. "Can I ask - just out of interest, why didn't you come back into the house the same way you left?"

Seymour seemed taken aback. "Um ... well, I don't really know. I suppose I could have ..." He took a deep breath. "I just didn't, sergeant. I suppose I probably didn't want to run into Horace. So I went round the back. If you don't believe me, ask Amelia. She'll tell you. Alright?"

"Not a problem sir," replied Copper calmly. "Absolutely no need to get belligerent. We just have to check everything. And we intend to have a word with Miss Cook anyway, so we can ask her then."

"Right. Sorry. I'm just a bit jumpy. It's all the questions."

"Well, sir, if you can just tell us what happened after you came back into the house, and then I imagine that we shan't need to ask you too many more. You say Miss Cook let you into the kitchen, and then what?"

"I went up to my room."

"And did you see anyone else on your way upstairs, sir?"

"No, because I went up the servants' stairs."

"What servants' stairs are these, sir? We haven't seen any stairs other than the main staircase in the hall."

Seymour smiled wanly. "This house has secrets, sergeant. You'd be surprised."

"I think we're finding that out, sir." And as Seymour's smile faded, "So perhaps you'd explain."

"There's a little door in the corner of the kitchen. It looks like a cupboard, but it leads to a tiny stair which goes right up through the house to the servants' rooms in the attic. They used to use it so that the servants didn't come face-to-face with the Lawdowns during the day, or for taking morning tea up to the bedrooms or what-have-you. So I just popped straight up there and came out through the door on the landing near my room. You wouldn't have noticed it – it's hidden in the panelling. And when I went in, there was Albert sitting on the bed. Actually, he made me jump out of my skin, because I was thinking of other things so of course I wasn't expecting anyone to be there."

Dave Copper made a show of consulting his notes. "Yes, sir, Mr. Ross mentioned that he spoke to you. Would you care to tell us what you remember of the conversation."

"He ... er ... well, it was just that he wanted a bit of advice about something." Seymour sounded evasive. "Family matters, I

122

think, but to be perfectly frank, sergeant, I tend not to listen too closely when Albert's talking. I'm afraid he does have a habit of droning on a bit, so I think I just gave him 'the soft answer that turneth away wrath', or whatever the saying is."

"And then?"

"And then we came back downstairs together, and went into the drawing room with Laura. And the dear girl had a life-saving bottle of scotch with her, so I'm afraid I didn't waste too much time in wrapping myself round some of that. So there we all were - oh, except for Robin Allday, but he turned up a couple of minutes after that - and there we all stayed. Apart from the vicar, of course, because Sandra asked him to go out and check on Horace about ten to one, and he came straight back and told us what he'd found."

Dave Copper snapped his notebook shut. "Which, of course, we've already heard in some detail, sir, so we shan't need you to go into that."

"So that's it?"

"For the moment, yes, Mr. Cummings," said Andy Constable. "So if you'd like to rejoin the others in the drawing room, please do, and I'd be grateful if you'd ask Mr. Allday if he could come through."

As Seymour escaped, Dave Copper raised an eyebrow in the direction of his superior. "I think Mr. Cummings was a lot more rattled about Horace Cope and what he knew than he was letting on, sir. What do you reckon?"

"I reckon that Mr. Cummings has a great deal to be rattled about, Copper. If his whole career was about to go down the pan, you can understand why. But you have to admit that he seemed pretty relieved when we told him that, as far as we can tell, the information, whatever it was, that Horace Cope held hadn't got as far as his editor. But I have trouble working out what Seymour Cummings is all about. For a man who was talking about being perfectly frank with us, getting information out of him first time round is like pulling teeth. And there's another thing I'm really not clear about."

"What's that, sir?"

"What's his relationship with Lady Lawdown? Or Laura Biding, for that matter. Is he just out for himself, or is he close enough to the family to kill in order to protect them from ...

123

whatever it was that Horace Cope knew. He knew something, that's obvious."

"Maybe Mr. Allday can help out on that front, sir."

And right on cue, a brisk knock at the door heralded Robin Allday's arrival. Inspector Constable indicated that he should take the seat in front of the desk, but then sat back, gazing over steepled fingers, for long moments. Robin, initially calm, began to fidget.

"I hope you won't think I'm being obstructive, inspector," he said, "but I'm sure you realise that there are rules about questioning people and the circumstances under which you do it, and I doubt that you would wish to step outside them. I'm not at all certain that it's proper to keep everyone cooped up next door for all this time. I'm sure you understand."

"Oh yes, I think I understand very well, Mr. Allday," replied Constable. "Of course, you will appreciate that there's been no question of coercing anybody at all. We've merely asked you and the others if you wouldn't mind remaining in the house for a time while we have a chat with each of you. After all, I'm sure everyone is as anxious as we are to clear up this business of Mr. Cope's death as quickly as possible. Why, has somebody made a complaint about our conduct?"

"Oh, not at all," said Robin hastily. "No, no, it's just that - well, people are becoming a little uneasy, not knowing what's going on, so I just said that I'd mention ..." He tailed off, then took a breath and resumed in a more confident tone. "So, inspector, how can I help you?"

"Rules, Mr. Allday."

"I'm sorry?"

Constable leaned forward across the desk and gazed steadily at Robin. "You spoke about rules, Mr. Allday. Funnily enough, Sergeant Copper and I were talking about rules a little while ago. And I believe you and I had something of a discussion about rules when we spoke earlier. Rules of your profession, I think, wasn't it?"

"Er, yes, I believe so."

"Anyway, sir, back to the matter in hand," said Constable briskly, rubbing his hands together. "Now, we've been asking people about their movements from around twelve o'clock, which is when Mr. Cope arrived on the premises. And, I understand, when you were due to arrive on the premises, but didn't."

"No, but I think I explained that to you before, inspector. I was invited for twelve, but I got held up at the office doing some paperwork. I'm sure I don't need to tell you how time-consuming paperwork is."

"Indeed sir. And ...?" Constable sat back and waited.

"And? Oh, yes, and I had to make a couple of phone calls which Laura had asked me to do."

"Miss Biding asked you to make some calls, did she, sir? Anything you'd like to tell us about those? If it's within the rules, of course."

Robin hesitated for a moment, then seemed to come to a decision, and sighed. "All right, inspector. I don't suppose the question of client confidentiality matters much now, so you may as well know that Horace had wanted me to put his new flat in London in Laura's name."

"Really, sir? And why did he ask you to do that? Did he explain?"

"He said something about it being a purely business arrangement."

"A business arrangement between Mr. Cope and Miss Biding? So how did that work out, sir?"

Robin flushed. "I really don't know anything at all about any arrangements, inspector. That wouldn't be any of my business. And as long as a property is correctly registered, there is no restriction on who actually pays for it. Why, has somebody implied that there is?"

"Not at all as far as we know, sir. I'm sure that you're far better informed on property law than we are," replied Constable smoothly. "But I'm grateful that you mentioned the matter, because it ties up a couple of loose ends. As it happens, we had already been told about a little exchange between you and Mr. Cope on the subject of this flat."

"What exchange? I hope you're not going to place too much reliance on what you may have been told about a private conversation between a solicitor and his client, inspector."

"I'm not sure to what extent talk overheard in a pub can be described as private conversation, Mr. Allday, but let's not pursue that point too closely."

"In any case," continued Robin, "it's all rather academic now, isn't it, because that particular property transaction won't be going through now, will it?"

"And possibly just as well, from what we gather from Miss Cook."

"Amelia?" Robin sounded baffled. "What on earth has Amelia got to do with it?"

"Oh, nothing at all, sir. It's just a bit of confirmation of what you told us about the proposed arrangement with Miss Biding over this flat. We had a chat with Miss Cook earlier, and she was able to fill us in with some helpful detail. But, as you say, that transaction won't be going through, so we won't need to look any more closely at it, will we?"

"No." Robin sounded relieved.

"At least, not that particular transaction." Robin's head came up sharply. "Anyway," said Constable, moving on before Robin could ask what he meant, "Let's talk about these phone calls which the young lady asked you to make. These were also about this same flat business, were they?"

"Er, yes, of course."

"So not relevant then, would you say?"

"To the murder, you mean? No, no, I can't see that they could be."

"So in that case, what was the other phone call about?"

"Other call?"

"Yes, Mr. Allday. You mentioned another phone call from Miss Biding. Copper?"

Dave Copper thumbed back through his notebook. "Yes, sir - got it here. You told us that Miss Biding called you this morning."

"Oh yes, of course. That. Yes, Laura phoned this morning - I suppose it must have been about twenty past twelve or so, I think I said. I'd totally lost track of time, and she called me to say she needed my help."

"Help, sir?"

Robin shifted in his chair uncomfortably. "With the guests, you know," he said. "Just ... well, keeping the conversation going, looking after the vicar, pouring oil, that sort of thing."

"Oil, sir?"

"On troubled waters." And in response to Copper's enquiring look, "I imagine you've been told by now, Horace could quite easily raise a few hackles, even when on the surface he was appearing to be at his most charming. In fact, especially when he was being charming."

"But Mr. Cope had left the gathering by the time Miss Biding called you, hadn't he, Mr. Allday?"

"But I wasn't to know that, was I? Anyway," he hurried on, "Laura phoned me, and I was at my office in the village which is only about five minutes away, so I dropped everything and drove up to the Hall straight away. I didn't bother to ring the bell when I got here - I just came in through the front door, because that one's never locked, and found everyone else in the drawing room."

Dave Copper consulted his notebook again. "Which would have been what time, sir?"

Robin gazed at the ceiling. "It would have been about ten minutes before Mr. Pugh went out to check on Horace, so it would have been about twenty to, I suppose. And I didn't leave until after he came back and told us what he'd found. And then I called 999."

"From in here, sir?" asked Andy Constable.

"Yes, inspector," replied Robin, puzzled. "Why do you ask?"

"No particular reason, sir," smiled Constable. "My colleague just likes to make sure all the details are correct. So if there's nothing else that strikes you, Copper ...?"

"No, sir."

" ... then I think we'll leave it at that for now. But if you'd ask Miss Biding to come in here, we can just verify this business about the phone calls and a few other things. Just to make sure all the details are correct. Right, Copper?"

As Robin Allday made his escape from the library, Andy Constable couldn't help laughing at the look of consternation on the solicitor's face. "And what, sergeant, is your assessment of Mr. Allday's state of mind at this present moment?" he asked.

"If you'll pardon the expression, sir, bricking it," responded Copper. "But at least we've got an explanation now for how that letter of his came to be here. I reckon he told Miss Biding about it when they spoke on the phone, and then he

127

brought it up here to show her. To try and work out what to do, I suppose. But ... how about this? He tells Miss Biding about the letter, but before he gets here, she nips out to put a stop to Horace's little plan, but they never get a chance to talk about it when he arrives because they're all together in the drawing room, so when the body gets found he dumps the letter in here when he phones us. And he thinks she's done it, and he's afraid of being brought in as an accessory!"

Andy Constable nodded approvingly. "Nice theory, sergeant. But there's one thing I'd like to know. If Miss Biding called him at twenty past, and he came straight here, which takes five minutes, how come he didn't arrive until twenty to? Did Mr. Allday find something unpleasant to do to fill in those missing minutes? Or has somebody got their timings wrong?" He smiled grimly. "Let's hope Miss Biding can help us."

*

Laura Biding took her place facing the inspector with an air of outward calm, belied by the hands which twisted together in her lap.

"We're sorry to have kept you waiting so long, Miss Biding," said Constable.

"That's perfectly all right, inspector," replied Laura. "I do understand that you need to find out everything that everybody knows if you are to discover who killed Uncle Horace."

"Hmmm," mused Constable. "Uncle Horace. And that's what you usually called him?"

"Yes," said Laura uncertainly.

"Not the ordinary uncle-niece relationship, though, was it? Even allowing for the fact that Mr. Cope wasn't actually your uncle, was he?"

"But I told you before, inspector, it was just a sort of courtesy title. It started when I was quite young. Everybody does it, don't they? I mean, you can't call your parents' old friends Mr. or Mrs. so-and-so, can you?"

"Ah, now we come to the other point, Miss Biding. Old friends. So you'd describe you and Mr. Cope as old friends too, would you?"

"I ... I suppose so. Why wouldn't I?"

"Well, there's the thing, Miss Biding. You see, from one or two things we hear, your relationship with Mr. Cope wasn't

128

entirely friendly, was it? In fact, we gather that there had been some tension between you and Mr. Cope only a couple of days ago. You met up, I believe, and had a conversation which wasn't exactly amicable? Didn't Mr. Cope make some suggestions which seemed to upset you? And weren't there some unfriendly remarks about your mother?"

Laura's calm exterior vanished. "Who the hell ...?" she exploded. "Oh, of course! Amelia! Blasted gossip! I might have known she'd be listening in. And what else did she tell you?"

Andy Constable hesitated. "I think we'll keep the rest of our conversation with Miss Cook private for the moment, Miss Biding," he said. "That is, unless there's any further information which you'd like to volunteer?"

"No." Although Laura flushed slightly, she pressed her lips together and seemed determined to say nothing further.

"Very well, Miss Biding. So let's move on to what happened this afternoon." Andy Constable turned to his colleague. "Copper, I think you've got some details you need to check up on."

"Right then, miss." Dave Copper opened his notebook again. "It's the timings, miss. Once we've got those clearly sorted out, then we can have a better idea of who had the opportunity to kill Mr. Cope. Sorry, 'Uncle Horace', if you prefer."

Laura snorted with irritation. "All right, sergeant, you've made your point. So maybe Uncle Horace wasn't quite the dear old family friend I said he was, but I couldn't have killed him, could I?"

"How so, miss?"

"For a start, you know where I was all the time. I was in the drawing room with Mother and the others to start with, and then I went out to get more drinks, but Helen was with me then, and after that I came in here to make a phone call to Robin Allday - you know all about that, I suppose?"

"We have been told about the call, yes, miss," confirmed Copper. "Whether we know all about it, I couldn't say."

"Oh ... right." Laura paused, disconcerted. "Anyway, after I spoke to Robin, I went back into the drawing room, and I didn't leave the room after that. And then Robin arrived a bit later, and then Mr. Pugh came back, but he went out again to open the gate to the Secret Garden at about ten to one. So that's it," she finished triumphantly.

"So then, Miss Biding," resumed Inspector Constable, "according to your reckoning, nobody could have murdered Mr. Cope?"

A sudden thought seemed to strike Laura. "Unless you count dear Mr. Pugh, of course. After all, he was the only one who went out to the Secret Garden on his own. Why don't you ask him if he did it?"

Chapter 12

"Do you know what, Copper," sighed Andy Constable, running his hands through his hair. "There are two things I'm getting heartily sick of."

"What's that, then, sir?"

"People not telling us the truth, and this damned library. I have the stupidest feeling that it's sitting here looking at me smugly, thinking 'Well, I know what happened, even if you don't'."

"If you don't mind me saying so, sir, isn't that just ever so slightly paranoid?"

Constable smiled. "You're absolutely right, sergeant. These people are driving me loopy."

"In which case, sir, I have a solution. I reckon it's all down to lack of fluids. What you need is a cup of tea."

"Oh hell!" Constable leapt to his feet. "Amelia Cook! She'll be hopping up and down. I promised we'd go and see her to find out what it was she was going on about. Come on, we'll kill two birds with one stone. We'll see if we can persuade her to make us some tea while we're at it."

As the two detectives emerged into the hall, P.C. Collins was just coming back through the front door.

"The vicar's safely back at the vicarage, sir," he reported. "Sorry I've been quite a time, but he would ask me in and insisted on making me a cup of tea. I don't know why it is, but people always seem to think that a policeman wants a cup of tea."

The inspector laughed. "That is because, Collins, on this occasion they would be absolutely right. Come on – you can come and join us in the kitchen for another cup, if you've got room, and a bit of Miss Cook's famous cake, if there's any left. And we'll make sure she doesn't blame you for us keeping her waiting and making her late." He pushed his way through the baize door from the hall and on into the kitchen, stopped short, and groaned.

Amelia Cook was seated at the table, a large rich fruit cake in front of her, with one inviting slice cut from it and

131

waiting on a doily-covered tea-plate next to it. As appetising as it looked, no-one was tempted to sample it, even though it was the last cake Amelia would ever bake. The cake-knife, gleaming stainless steel with an antler handle, protruded from the side of her neck where it had been driven down into her chest.

Dave Copper was already on the phone as Andy Constable stepped forward to take a closer look at the body. Ignoring the murmured words in the background – 'another one', 'bit late for an ambulance', 'get SOCO back here' – the inspector beckoned Collins forward. "Come and take a look at this, lad."

"Do I really have to, sir?"

Constable smiled grimly. "First body, is it?"

Collins nodded.

"Then you absolutely do have to, son. This is why we do our job, and the more you know, and the sooner you know it, the better you get. Just remember not to touch her – we'd better leave all that to the doctor. So, what do you see?"

"Well, she's been stabbed, sir. Sorry, sir – that sounds stupid."

"It's not stupid at all, Collins. It might be obvious, but if I told you the number of cases where people have got things wrong by overlooking the obvious, you'd be amazed. So come on – what can you tell?"

As the young P.C. wrinkled his forehead in concentration, Dave Copper moved forward but the inspector waved him back, mouthing 'Give him a chance'. "She's just sat there," said Collins, "so she can't have been expecting it. I mean, if she'd been having a row with somebody, she'd have been up and about, or facing them. It looks as if whoever did this was behind her."

"Good thinking, Collins. And so ...?"

"So ..." Collins spoke slowly as the thoughts formed in his mind. "So she must have known whoever it was, and trusted them. I mean, if you're worried about someone, you don't let them prowl about behind you with a knife in their hand, do you?"

"You don't. So, a friend, then?"

"But that could mean anybody, sir. And why would they do it? Everybody in the village liked Amelia – I've never heard

132

anyone say a bad word about her."

"Fortunately, we don't have to worry about everybody in the village," remarked Constable drily. "I'm assuming we only have to worry about the people in this house. Providing that the kitchen back door's still locked, Copper," he said, as a sudden thought struck him.

"Yes sir. Solid as a rock, and the key's still here in the lock."

"So just our six, then. Copper, you'd better go through to the drawing room and make sure that they're all still there. If somebody's done a runner, we might have a bit of a clue as to who's done this. In any event, tell them they're going to have to sit tight for a while longer."

"Shall I tell them what's happened, sir?"

"Best not for the moment," replied Constable. "Just tell them there's been a development – a bit of a complication. You never know, it might make whoever was responsible a bit jumpier, and when people get jumpy they make mistakes."

As the door closed behind the sergeant, Andy Constable turned back to Collins. "So then, lad, what else have we got?"

"I've been thinking, sir," said Collins. "The cake and the knife, sir. I reckon I know what must have happened. Someone's come in here, sir, and they've been talking to Amelia, and she's cut them a bit of cake – no, she offered them some cake, so they've cut themselves a slice, and then, while they've still got the knife in their hand, they've gone round behind her and stabbed her."

"Spur of the moment?"

"I think it must have been, sir. If you're going to come in here intending to kill someone, you're sort of going to come prepared, aren't you? Not just grab a handy cake-knife. But I still don't see why."

"Think it through, Collins. Why do people kill people? Come on, you've covered this sort of stuff in your training."

"Well, there's all the obvious things, sir, like domestic violence or robberies that go wrong."

"Which is obviously not the case here."

"So what, then, sir?"

"Threat, Collins. People kill people because they're a threat to them."

"But sir," objected Collins, "how could Amelia be a threat to somebody? She was just a nice old lady – she wouldn't have hurt a fly. All right, she was a bit of a gossip, but that's not going to be a reason to kill someone, is it?"

Inspector Constable smiled grimly. "You know, Collins, that's exactly where you're wrong. Threats aren't always physical, you know. Very often it's what somebody knows about you that is the threat – to your position, to your career, to your family. And that's just the sort of threat that's pushed our murderer over the edge."

"Murderer, sir? Singular? So you reckon whoever did this is the one that killed Horace Cope?"

"I think the chances of having two separate murderers in the same house on the same afternoon is stretching coincidence a bit too far, Collins," replied the inspector. "Look at the similarities. The attack came from behind. So somebody the victim knew and had no reason to fear. Somebody who probably didn't set out to kill, but grabbed the opportunity with what was to hand. You had it right when you said whoever it was had been talking to Amelia. Or rather, she was talking to them. She said something which proved that she knew the reason why Horace Cope had been killed. And so she got herself killed into the bargain. She may not even have realised exactly what it was she knew, or why it was dangerous." He shook his head in frustration. "Poor silly woman."

"But how do you find out what it was that she knew, sir?" asked Collins.

"Oh, she's already told us, Collins. I'm sure of that. The only trouble is, she's told us too much."

"How do you mean, sir?"

"Sergeant Copper and I have been talking to our suspects while you were taking the vicar back to the village. We've had them all in the library, one by one, and we've winkled out a few things which they weren't too eager to tell us about first off." Constable snorted. "You will learn in this job, Collins, if you haven't learnt it already, that the world is full of people who are stupid enough to think that you're stupid, so they think they can get away with not telling you the truth. Anyway, it turns out that pretty much all of that lot next door had had some sort of trouble with Horace Cope which Amelia

Cook had overheard or seen or been told about. We'd had a very long chat with her earlier on, and it came as a bit of a surprise to a few people as to what we knew. Put a few cracks into a few people's stories. So every one of them left the library with some reason not to be too pleased with Miss Cook."

"And the murderer was afraid that what Amelia knew would lead you to them, sir? Is that it?"

"That's exactly it, Collins. One of them has come in here after leaving us, and they've ended up making sure that Miss Cook didn't tell us any more than she already had. And then it looks as if they've calmly gone back in to join the others in the drawing room."

The door to the passage opened, and Dave Copper put his head into the kitchen. "SOCO are on their way back, sir. They reckon they shouldn't be long."

Inspector Constable took a deep breath. "Right, then – we'll let them get on with it. Not that I expect they'll tell us much we haven't already figured out. Collins, you'd better stay here until they arrive and bring them in here. Come on, Copper – back to the library." He led the way into the hall.

As the two detectives sank back into the leather sofas flanking the library fireplace, Andy Constable gave a profound sigh.

"I'm depressed, Copper."

"Any particular reason, sir? That is, apart from the fact that we've got two dead bodies?"

Constable smiled ruefully. "You're right, Copper – that does tend to put a bit of a damper on things. No, I mean that I get demoralised when a bunch of people who seem so pleasant on the surface turn out to have a whole bunch of skeletons in the cupboard. I'm sure everybody was nicer when I was a kid."

"Doesn't it sort of come with the territory, sir? I mean, haven't you got used to that by now? After all, it's what we deal with, every day."

"You're right of course, sergeant, but it doesn't mean I have to like it." He gave a slight shake as if to pull himself together. "So, let's think. First things first. We need to figure out which of our suspects had the strongest motive for wishing Horace Cope out of the way."

"He had something on all of them, by the looks of it, sir,

so that's not going to be easy," remarked Copper.

"True, but it's all tied up with the various things he had – the documents and so on."

"And the book, sir, and the stuff on his computer – remember the photo file I couldn't open, and that email."

"Don't worry, I haven't forgotten any of that. I should like to have taken a look at those photos, just to confirm what I'm already thinking, but I've got a pretty strong idea what we'd find. Remember that newspaper clipping. I think we can make a good guess as to who 'L' is."

"And the email?" persisted Copper.

"Well, it's fairly obvious what was going on there," responded the inspector. "The only question there is whether Seymour Cummings knew what was going on or not. He seemed surprised when we mentioned it, so either he didn't have a clue about it, or else he's a pretty good actor. But then what led him to have that row which Amelia overheard? What else had Horace Cope done that we maybe don't know about? Either way, Mr. Cummings isn't out of it by any means."

Dave Copper frowned. "I still don't see what the point of that letter is, sir – you know, the one from the Family Records Office. All that does is mention two more people, and we haven't got a clue who they are."

"Not strictly true, Copper," said Constable. "You don't get all that many people called Biding, so it's a reasonable assumption that Rex Biding is related to Laura Biding. But I don't know – father? Brother?"

"Can't be brother, sir," interrupted Copper. "She told us she was an only child."

"So far as she knows. Maybe not. But if it is her brother, what's happened to him? But all right, then, let's say father. So at some point, this Rex Biding was married to Alexandra Thyme, whoever she may be, so that means ... what? Is Laura Biding their daughter and not Lady Lawdown's? Is that what they're trying to hide? Or was Rex Biding married to someone else before he met Lady Lawdown, so is Laura illegitimate? You wouldn't necessarily want the world to know that either."

"I wish I could have got into that safe for you, sir," said Copper ruefully. "I bet that certificate's in there, and it might have told us. Mind you, I do have a few contacts who could get into a safe like that in a couple of minutes, but I don't suppose the higher-ups would be too keen on their methods."

Andy Constable held up a hand, smiling. "If you don't mind, Copper, we'll just stick to procedures on this one. I think we'd better leave some of your more disreputable underworld friends out of the picture. Anyway, the point is, there's some family secret there."

"And the book, sir? You know, the new Carrie Otter. Actually, I wouldn't mind having a read of that, if we don't need it for anything. I can't really see why we should."

"And your reasoning would be ...?"

"Well, he was a book critic, wasn't he, sir?" said Copper. "So he had a book to review. And Helen Highwater told us she got it for him."

"Ah, but if you remember, Amelia Cook said that he turned down her offer to do so. So which of them is right?"

"Could be both, sir," pointed out Copper. "He changed his mind, so she got him the book because she was still trying to get round him so that he would give her a good review."

"You know, Copper, the way you and the rest of the world seem addicted to Carrie Otter, I can't see that one review either way is going to make a lot of difference to the lady."

Dave Copper thought for a moment. "So then there's Robin Allday's letter. I don't see how he could be any deeper in it than he already is. Mind you, I suppose it all depends on what Horace Cope had already told them about what he'd been up to."

"That, Copper," remarked Andy Constable, "is to assume that Horace Cope was the one who had made the allegations to the Law Society. We can't be absolutely certain that it was."

"No, sir, but it's a reasonable assumption, isn't it?" said Copper. "We know from what Gideon Porter overheard that Horace Cope at least thought he knew that Robin had been up to some dodgy practices, and we know from the email to Seymour Cummings' editor that Horace wasn't above shoving people in the shi... er ... mire, if it meant he could get his own way. But we still don't know how much Horace had told them, so maybe Robin thought he could stop the whole story getting out if he could put Horace out of the way in time. But what's he doing bringing that letter up here?"

137

Andy Constable leaned forward in thought. "I think he brought it here to show to Laura Biding," he said slowly, "in the hope that she'd be able to help him somehow. It's obvious that Robin's got a soft spot for her, even if she may not know it, and she's evidently involved in this business about the London flat, so maybe he thought he could get her to wheedle her way around Horace Cope so that he'd change his mind about putting Robin in it. So they figured out something together. And the letter got dumped in the bin here because they weren't thinking straight in the panic of the moment. Or else ..." A thought seemed to strike him. "Or else he showed it to Laura, she realised that Horace was an even nastier piece of work than she already knew, and she killed Horace because he was a threat to Robin, for whom she had a soft spot." He held his head in his hands. "You know, Copper, all these motives are likely to drive me mad. I shouldn't be surprised if we end up finding that everybody killed him."

"Sorry to add to your woes, sir, but you haven't mentioned those kitchen gloves I found in the Secret Garden."

"Well, Copper, that's the one bright spot in the whole case. I reckon we can be pretty sure of getting some DNA off the inside of those, so with a bit of luck it'll be clear enough to tell us who last wore them." He sighed. "That's as long as it wasn't Amelia Cook, of course. That would really screw things up."

"No problem there, then, sir," replied Copper confidently. "You don't wear kitchen gloves to do the cooking. They'd get in the way. But anyway, we're not going to get those results just yet, and then you're going to need to get samples from everyone, so it's going to take a time to get it sorted that way, isn't it?"

"You're right, sergeant. We're going to have to get by for the moment on the evidence we've already got. Of which we don't appear to have a shortage."

At that moment there was a tap at the library door, and P.C. Collins put his head into the room.

"Sorry to interrupt you, sir, ..."

"That's all right, Collins. Come on in. What is it?"

"A couple of things, sir." He held out an object towards the inspector. "The scouts clearing up rubbish in the grounds have found this key." The small brass object glinted wetly in his hand. "They found it in the long grass just outside the gate to the Secret Garden, and one of them had the thought of trying it in the lock there, and they found it fitted, but they didn't like to bring it into the house that way, what with everything that had gone on, so they came round to the front door with it. I'm afraid they've all been mauling it about," he added apologetically, "so there's not much chance of getting any prints off it. I would have ticked them off about that, sir, but I thought it was quite bright of them to bring it to me."

"Terrific!" responded the inspector. "Another bit of evidence! Just what I was hoping for!" He turned to the sergeant. "So, Copper, what do you reckon? Helpful or unhelpful?"

"It all depends how it got there, doesn't it, sir," replied Copper. "As far as I can see, you've got three possibilities. Seymour Cummings might have dropped it by accident when he went out for his walk this morning. Or it's possible that whoever killed Horace Cope isn't still in the house at all, and they let themselves out of the Secret Garden gate after killing him and chucked the key down as they left."

"Yes, but that's not really likely, is it," objected Constable. "For a start, if the murderer wore the rubber gloves, they wouldn't dump them in the garden and then use the key with bare hands, would they? It would be too much of a risk. And anyway, we've got quite enough suspects without dragging in half the villagers who were setting up the fete. So what's your third option?"

"The murderer might have come in through the gate, done the murder, and then thrown the key over the wall to make it look as if they'd gone out rather than coming in."

"Except, sergeant, that the only person we know of who was outside with the key was Seymour Cummings, and he had to get Amelia Cook to let him back into the house through the kitchen back door."

"So he says, sir."

P.C. Collins cleared his throat. "I'm sorry if I've mucked things up, sir. I didn't realise that the key would make things more complicated. I thought it would help." He looked downcast.

"That's fine, Collins," said Constable. "Don't worry about

it. You did exactly the right thing. I'm just getting grouchy. You're probably right about the fingerprints on the key, but it won't do any harm to let SOCO have it."

"That was the other thing, sir," said Collins. "SOCO have arrived and they've been working on things in the kitchen, and they've taken a look in Amelia Cook's handbag. It was hanging on a hook on the back of the door under her coat, which is why nobody noticed it before. But they've found this piece of paper with something written on it, and they wondered if it might be relevant."

Collins handed the folded paper to the inspector. On it were written just a few words in Amelia's spidery old-lady hand. Constable read them, then took a deep breath, closed his eyes, and gave a long sigh.

"What does it say, sir?" enquired Dave Copper.

"It says, 'She gets smothered in the end', sergeant," replied Andy Constable. He paused for several long moments, gazing unfocussed into the fireplace, and then stood, his eyes darkening. "Come on, Copper. Let's finish this."

"What, sir?" Dave Copper was startled. "Do you reckon you've got it? Just like that?"

"Yes, sergeant," replied Constable grimly. "Just like that." He led the way from the room.

Chapter 13

The atmosphere in the Drawing Room of Dammett Hall was profoundly gloomy, hardly relieved at all by the two table lamps which had been turned on to counteract the steady fading of the daylight, as the rain poured down outside from low charcoal clouds. Sandra Lawdown rose.

"I hope very much, inspector," she said with a sort of nervous haughtiness, "that you have come to tell us that you have finished with us at last."

"In many respects, your ladyship, yes," replied Constable.

"Thank heavens for that. I know you've had your duty to do, inspector, but for the rest of us, life has to go on, and I for one need to make some arrangements. For a start, someone has to organise a meal for this evening." She took a step towards the door.

"I'm sorry, my lady, but that won't be possible just at the moment," said Constable. "Please take a seat." And, forestalling the words of protest which were already forming on Lady Lawdown's lips, "I'm afraid you won't be able to use your kitchen for some time, not until my colleagues have finished in there. It is now being examined as a crime scene. I have to tell you that Miss Amelia Cook has been murdered."

Gasps and murmurs of shock rose all round the room, as Lady Lawdown sank on to a sofa. "Amelia murdered?" she said with an effort. "But how? When? Who would have ..." She tailed off in seeming bewilderment, as Laura Biding came to sit alongside her and put an arm round her shoulder.

"Inspector," said Laura, "Do you mean that Amelia's been killed by the same person who killed Uncle Horace."

"It appears so, miss."

"And you think you know who it is?"

"I believe so, miss."

Seymour Cummings could not contain himself any longer. "This is ridiculous, man!" he barked. "Are you trying to tell us that there's some sort of lunatic assassin going about? In Dammett Worthy, of all places? The idea's absurd."

"I grant you that, sir," replied Constable. "On the face of it, Dammett Worthy is the perfect English village. So who would have thought that it was such a hotbed of secrets? Oh yes," he said in response to the murmur of protest which arose from the six as they exchanged uneasy glances. "The difficulty of an investigation like this is that during the course of it, we tend to uncover so many secrets, even among the innocent, that we can have something of a problem sorting the wheat from the chaff. And who would have thought that such a popular character as Horace Cope could have so many enemies?"

"How could Horace have had enemies, inspector?" protested Albert Ross. "I've never heard of such a thing. He was a fine man, a fine journalist and an outstanding clairvoyant – he was a visionary."

"Well, let's not overdo things, Mr. Ross," said Constable. "He may have been all those things, but I can assure you that, from what we've learnt, he did have enemies. People over whom he had a hold, because of what he knew about them. Now that may be the way to influence people, but it's certainly not the way to make friends. So I have to ask myself, how come Mr. Cope didn't foresee the trouble he was storing up for himself? Perhaps it's because he wasn't a very good clairvoyant." He permitted himself a small dry smile.

"You said something about people's secrets," said Helen Highwater.

"I did, Miss Highwater. Because we've discovered that what Horace Cope was very good at, was getting hold of other people's secrets and using them for his own ends. Yes, even against his own cousin, the only other member of his family. Because he had Albert Ross round his neck, sponging off him all the time, cluttering up his house and showing no signs of wanting to move on."

Albert Ross jumped to his feet. "That is simply not true, inspector," he riposted with an unusual display of vehemence. "I've told you, Horace was very good to me, and I will not have him insulted in this fashion. Horace was a great believer in family loyalty, you take my word for it."

"Sit down, Mr. Ross," said Constable wearily. "I wish we could take your word for it, but I'm afraid that from what we've been told from sources that we're quite happy to rely on, family

142

loyalty was not exactly in plentiful supply in Mr. Cope's household. Oh, I don't doubt that you had quite a cushy number for quite a while, but I think you went and blotted your copybook, didn't you?"

"I really don't understand you," muttered Albert uneasily.

"Oh, I think you do, Mr. Ross," replied Constable. "And in fact, if there was any possibility that hearsay evidence might stand up in court, we might well want to have a long talk with you about certain antique items which went missing from Mr. Cope's cottage. And possibly even some other pieces of silver which disappeared a little closer to hand."

Lady Lawdown looked up. "What?" she said sharply. "Do you mean the silver we had stolen from the Hall? Are you trying to tell us that Albert was responsible for that?"

"I'm not trying to tell you anything, my lady," responded Constable. "I can't spare the time to think about that incident just at the moment. We have more important things on our minds. But it may well have been on Mr. Ross's mind. It seems that Mr. Cope was just about to pull the plug on his cousin. Albert Ross was about to be thrown out on to the streets." And as Albert seemed to be about to protest again, "Please don't deny it, Mr. Ross. We are pretty sure of our facts. So what I have to consider is, did you take drastic action to turn yourself from an unwelcome guest into the owner of a very comfortable home, as Horace Cope's only heir?"

As Albert sat there stunned and silent, Andy Constable turned to Laura Biding.

"Miss Biding, you told us quite a lot about your ... what did you call him? Your 'Uncle Horace'."

"Yes," said Laura impatiently, "but of course you know he wasn't actually my uncle. That was just what I'd always called him. I don't know what you're trying to imply. I've explained all that."

"Indeed you have, Miss Biding," soothed the inspector. "We aren't implying anything other than that he was an old friend of the family as you told us. But of course, that's just it. If Horace Cope wasn't too free with his expressions of family loyalty within his own family, there would be no reason to suppose that that loyalty would extend to anyone who wasn't family, would there? Now you started out telling us all about your dear generous Uncle Horace, but you've changed your tune since then, haven't you?"

Lady Lawdown looked at her daughter. "Laura ...?"

"Oh Mummy," sighed Laura, "you don't know the half of it."

"Darling, what is Mr. Constable driving at? What does he mean, you've changed your tune? Inspector, what on earth are you talking about?"

"I'm afraid it's all a little delicate, Lady Lawdown. You see, we have to consider the question of lifestyle."

Sandra Lawdown seemed baffled. "What lifestyle? Whose?"

"Ah, well, there you have it, my lady. In fact, it seems that the whole business is tied into the question of lifestyle. Not just Mr. Cope's, but everybody in this room. But I think we'll stay with yours, Miss Biding, for the moment. Now, you don't have a job, do you?"

"No," replied Laura, surprised. "Why do you ask?"

"Sometimes it's helpful to know people's sources of income, miss," said Constable blandly. "It can be relevant."

"Well, if you must know, although I can't see why you should, I have an allowance from a trust which was set up for me by my stepfather, Lord Lawdown."

"I assume it must be quite a generous one, miss, if it enables you to run that very smart little car of yours." And as Laura did not reply, "Which is probably as well, because it seems that the estate these days doesn't have a great deal of spare money at its disposal. I think that's correct, isn't it, your ladyship? From what we've been told."

"And who, may I ask, has been bandying my private business around?" demanded Sandra Lawdown. "Has Amelia been gossiping again, as usual? Is that what this is all about? Do you suppose I killed her because she let some sort of cat out of the bag about my financial state?"

"Oh Sandra," said Helen Highwater, "I'm so sorry. I think I was probably the one who told the inspector that money was a little tight for you. But I didn't mean anything by it. I never thought for a moment that it would cause trouble for dear Laura..." She tailed off.

144

Inspector Constable turned back to Laura. "So, miss, an allowance. Would that be your only income?"

Laura seemed oddly evasive. "I do a little modelling work from time to time, inspector."

Helen Highwater seemed eager to recover lost ground. "Oh inspector, Laura shouldn't be so modest. She's been in several of the fashion magazines, and she looked absolutely gorgeous on that cover of 'County Living'. I'm sure there's a copy here somewhere if you'd like to see."

"We'll leave that for the moment, Miss Highwater, I think. But we'll agree that Miss Biding is a very attractive young lady. Perhaps that's one of the reasons why Mr. Cope was so generous in taking her out dining or to the theatre. I'm sure many middle-aged men in the public eye are always happy to be seen out and about with a glamorous young woman. But it seems that Mr. Cope went rather further than that, didn't he? There was talk of him putting the flat he was planning to buy in London in your name, wasn't there, miss?"

"Laura, darling? Is that true?" Lady Lawdown seemed taken aback at the revelation. "But why on earth would Horace do that?"

"I'm sure the inspector is about to tell us, Mummy," said Laura wearily.

"The only thing we are certain of," continued Constable, "is that Horace Cope was overheard to mention the possibility that Miss Biding might use the flat for 'business'."

"What, staying in London when you went up to do modelling shoots, is that it, darling? Well, inspector, what's wrong with that?"

"Not a thing, my lady, if that is in fact what was proposed. Of course, there are other interpretations of the word 'business'. Are there not, Miss Biding? And based on a newspaper cutting which we found in the dead man's wallet, which mentioned the personal services of a certain lady called 'L', we could easily draw conclusions as to what 'business' Miss Biding was engaged in."

Laura glared defiantly at the inspector. "You have not a shred of proof of any of this wild tale," she declared. "If you dare to repeat any of this publicly, I will take you to court. Robin ...?" She looked to Robin Allday for confirmation.

145

"That may not be advisable, Miss Biding," replied Constable. "You see, there is a file of photographs which we have discovered on Mr. Cope's computer which may be of interest to us. Of course, it may not be relevant, but we shan't know that until we get past the security and open it up. Which we shall be doing if we think we need to."

Laura subsided. She sounded resigned. "I don't think you need trouble to do that, inspector. But I've done nothing illegal, and I resent this dragging out of my private life in front of everyone. It has nothing whatever to do with you."

"Ah, but it has, Miss Biding. Because I spoke of secrets, and here is one which I'm sure some people would go to almost any lengths to preserve. To protect their reputation. To protect their name, their family. It's very much a secret worth killing for." He turned to Laura's mother. "Is it not, your ladyship?"

Sandra Lawdown, who had been gazing at her daughter in horrified silence, rallied. "Are you trying to imply, inspector, that I knew all about this … whatever it is you believe Laura has done … and that I killed Horace in order to protect the family name? Is that seriously what you are suggesting?"

"I'm afraid it's rather more complicated than that, my lady," said Constable. "No, I don't see that you would have killed Horace Cope for your daughter's sake. But for all that, you were none too fond of him yourself, if the truth were told." And as Sandra Lawdown seemed about to protest, "No, please don't try to deny it. We've heard of one or two conversations between you which were not entirely friendly. And as lady of the manor and a Justice of the Peace, who knows, perhaps you even thought he was a little beneath you. And I'm sorry to have to tell you that behind your back, Mr. Cope was sometimes less than complimentary about you. In fact, the late Miss Cook overheard Mr. Cope saying that you were no lady. So how would you respond to that?"

Lady Lawdown remained looking straight ahead, lips firmly pressed together. Under the flawless make-up, her face seemed suddenly haggard.

"I mentioned some of the interesting items we discovered at Mr. Cope's cottage," continued Constable. "One of them was a letter from the Family Records Office which referred to a marriage certificate between a Mr. Rex Biding and

146

a Miss Alexandra Thyme. The certificate itself wasn't there – no doubt it's safely locked away in Mr. Cope's safe. So the question we then had to ask was, why was Mr. Cope so interested in it? Was that all of a piece with his professed interest in the records held at St. Salyve's church? Now I think we are safe in the assumption that Rex Biding is Laura's father. So then what about this marriage? Who was Alexandra Thyme? Was Lady Lawdown trying to hide the fact that she was never married to Laura's father, and that Laura is therefore illegitimate?"

Lady Lawdown sprang to her feet, provoked into fury. "Inspector, how dare you? That is the most insulting ..."

Andy Constable held up his hand to stem the flow. "Please allow me to finish, your ladyship. As I was about to say ..." He waited until Sandra Lawdown had resumed her seat. "We of course had the answer to that question almost before it had been asked. Because according to the vicar, when Mr. Cope and Lady Lawdown met in the church porch, Mr. Cope called her 'Alex'. Which might be thought strange, since her name is Sandra. But of course, it isn't strange at all, is it, my lady? It's simply that Alex is short for Alexandra, just as Sandra is short for Alexandra."

"Of course it is," said Lady Lawdown with more assurance. "I just happen to prefer the name Sandra. And I'm sure Horace used the name Alex purely to provoke me, although I have no idea why. He always had a spiteful streak. So I really cannot imagine what relevance all this has, inspector. What on earth does it matter what I call myself?"

"I think it matters a great deal, my lady," replied Constable. "You see, I haven't told you what else the letter said. Yes, there was a mention of Rex Biding's marriage. But what Horace Cope had asked for, and failed to get, was a copy of Rex Biding's death certificate. So why would he be interested in that? And why would the Family Records Office not be able to trace it? Their archives are pretty comprehensive, I understand. So the only thought that occurs to me is, perhaps this document didn't come to light because it doesn't exist. And perhaps Mr. Biding, whatever his daughter and other people may have been told, did not die when Laura was very young. Perhaps he did not die at all. So could it be that Lady Lawdown, J.P., is seeking to conceal the fact, not of illegitimacy, but of bigamy?"

Laura had been listening to the unfolding revelations with mounting incredulity. "Mummy ... I don't understand. Is the inspector telling us that daddy isn't dead? But you always told me that he died when I was a child." And in response to her mother's continuing silence, "Mummy, tell me!"

"Oh darling, I wish I could," answered Sandra Lawdown in a broken voice. "Your father ..." She turned to Andy Constable. "You're right of course, inspector. Rex was Laura's father. I suppose we were just too young. Laura was born a year after we married, and when she was two, I discovered that Rex was involved with another woman. In fact, several other women. I confronted him – he didn't deny it. So I told him to leave, and he did. I never saw him again."

"And did you not get a divorce?" asked Constable.

"No, inspector, I did not," said Lady Lawdown, recovering a little of her spirit. "I refused to undergo the embarrassment. And I wanted to protect Laura as best I could. So I just told her that her daddy had gone away. Later on, when she was old enough to ask questions, I told her that he had died. You may think that was cruel, but I thought it was no more cruel than letting her find out the sort of man her father really was. So the story was that Rex was dead. And as the years went by, I suppose I even came to believe it myself. And then I met Peter."

"That's Lord Lawdown?"

"Yes. And he was charming, and kind ... so when he asked me to marry him, what could I do? I wanted the best for Laura, so I put my past life behind me."

"So Rex Biding is still alive then?" said Constable.

"I really have no idea, inspector." She smiled through emerging tears and rose to her feet. "And look at everything I have. Look at this house. My title, my position – everything is built on a lie."

"And Horace Cope found out. How?"

Sandra Lawdown laughed bitterly. "He was a clairvoyant, inspector. Perhaps he divined it. How am I supposed to know? But he knew, and he let me know that he knew. Oh, nothing was ever said directly – he was too sly for that. And I don't know what he hoped to gain by the knowledge. But if you ask me if I'm sorry that he's dead, no, I'm not. I'm only sorry that the horrible truth didn't die with him. I would have given anything to spare my friends the knowledge that I'm a liar and a fraud. But I am not a murderer."

"And if that is the case, your ladyship, then there would probably be no need for the police to intrude further into your private affairs. Officially, that is. It may come as a surprise to some people, but we are sometimes capable of letting sleeping dogs lie, you know. So perhaps the matter of your past actions, and what you intend to do about them, is more a matter for your conscience than this investigation."

Seymour Cummings walked over to Sandra Lawdown and wrapped his arms around her in a wordless hug, as Helen Highwater dabbed her eyes with a handkerchief from her sleeve.

"Sandra," said Helen, "Don't worry that any of this will make a difference to us. We love you for the person we know you are."

"Thank you, Helen," said Lady Lawdown. "You are a true friend."

"Indeed, Miss Highwater," said Constable. "Some might say that you appear to be Lady Lawdown's best friend. And despite that friendship, or perhaps even because of it, you have had your own troubles with Horace Cope, haven't you?"

"In what way, troubles, inspector? I don't know what you mean."

"But you've told us about them yourself, Miss Highwater. Don't you remember? Of course, you're a very successful author, and your books have made you very wealthy, haven't they?"

Helen reddened slightly. "I won't deny it, inspector, I've been very lucky, and I must admit that I'm really quite comfortably off. But I don't see what that has to do with Horace's death."

"Ah, but the thing about wealth, Miss Highwater, is that it attracts all sorts of vultures. And it seems to me that Horace Cope might very well have been one of those vultures. Perhaps picking over the corpses."

"Corpses? What corpses?" retorted Helen sharply.

"Forgive me, Miss Highwater," said Constable. "Perhaps that wasn't a particularly tasteful expression. I was referring to your 'Carrie Otter' novels. Because Horace Cope had been none too complimentary about them in his newspaper column, had he? But I dare say you hoped for better in his review of your new book. On the other hand, of course, there is the fear that Mr. Cope might have used his column to give you more bad publicity. We can't tell, can we? So I imagine that it may be something of a mixed blessing that his final review will never appear in print. Will it?"

"No, inspector," agreed Helen quietly, "it won't."

Andy Constable steepled his fingers and tapped them together. "Mind you," he said, "there's one thing that I can't quite resolve. It's this question of Mr. Cope's possession of a copy of your final 'Carrie Otter' book. You told us that you gave it to him. Amelia Cook heard him decline your offer. And she also heard him make various other odd remarks which didn't sound particularly friendly."

Helen's tone grew waspish. "I'm sorry, inspector, but I'm becoming a little tired of people being accused of goodness-knows-what on the basis of Amelia Cook's bits and pieces of tittle-tattle. I don't like to speak ill of the dead, but I'm surprised that you pay so much attention to things half-heard from a woman who was probably only paying half-attention."

"Really, Miss Highwater? Well, whatever else may be true about Miss Cook, I think it is generally agreed that her cooking was usually very well appreciated. So shall we say that she was paying close enough attention to notice that, whatever it was that Horace Cope said, it was enough to put you off your food."

Chapter 14

Robin Allday stepped forward and cleared his throat. "Inspector, if I may interrupt, I think you are beginning to adopt something of a hectoring tone, and I'm not sure to what end. You seem to be intent on accusing each of us in turn of having some sort of motive for killing Horace."

"That is exactly my point, Mr. Allday," answered Constable. "When I was a young sergeant, my old inspector said to me, 'Know the man and you know his murderer'. So we've been looking at the character of Horace Cope, and we find that he loved to uncover people's secrets. And those secrets are what tell us the motives for murder. And I have to remind you that each and every person in this room had a motive to kill Horace Cope."

"Are you serious, inspector?"

"Sadly I am, sir. In fact, I think I would say that in your case, the motive is so obvious that if it weren't so serious, it would be laughable."

"I'm glad I'm providing you with some amusement, gentlemen," said Robin in acid tones. "So perhaps you'd like to tell me exactly what you're talking about."

"Very well, sir. Since you're so determined. Horace Cope was blackmailing you, wasn't he?"

A murmur of astonishment ran around the room.

"Sorry to put it in such shocking terms, Mr. Allday, but I shouldn't have thought that such an action on Mr. Cope's part would come as much of a surprise to anyone here. Now I have a bit of a problem with you, Mr. Allday, because I haven't a single piece of concrete evidence to go on. All I've got is hearsay." And as Robin seemed about to interrupt, "Quite a lot of hearsay, sir. Now you were about to put through a property transaction for Mr. Cope, weren't you? But some of the details look as if they may have involved sailing a bit close to the wind. You admitted as much to us yourself. But as you also pointed out, that particular deal isn't going to be taking place, so you don't seem to have a problem there. On the face of it. But why would you put yourself in such a position? Well, according to a conversation we've been told about by Gideon Porter, you'd done something of the sort before."

"You cannot know that, inspector," retorted Robin, "and if you haven't any evidence, I think you should be very careful about what you say in front of witnesses."

Andy Constable smiled affably. "How right you are, Mr. Allday. Well, I say no evidence, but of course, there's that letter to you from the Law Society, isn't there? Rather silly to leave that lying about."

Laura Biding's hand went to her mouth. "Oh Robin! I'm so sorry. I meant to ..."

"Laura." Robin Allday's voice held a warning tone. He turned back to the inspector. "So, yes, there is a letter. Which you obviously have. But I think you'll find that it makes no mention of Horace Cope. So in what way is this evidence?"

"Not evidence in itself, I grant you, sir," replied Constable, "but I think I'm as capable of putting two and two together as the next man. So here's Horace Cope, heard to threaten you with professional exposure because of what he has discovered, who knows how. Here are you, apparently agreeing to undertake activities which may threaten your career. Now why would you do that if there were no truth in his suspicions? Here's a letter which summons you to explain allegations of inappropriate conduct. Who wouldn't come to the conclusion that, although the source of the allegations isn't mentioned, Horace Cope was at the bottom of them? So has Horace Cope spilt the beans and done the damage already, or is he about to reveal the whole shocking truth, and stop your career dead in its tracks? Is your motive for killing Mr. Cope revenge, or did you kill him to stop the truth emerging? You tell me, Mr. Allday."

Robin subsided into a chair. "Nothing," he insisted. "You have nothing."

"Well, sir, we'll just have to wait until Monday morning to see what we have, shan't we," responded Constable easily. "I presume there won't be much point in calling on the Law Society before then. So we'll have a little chat with them when their offices open. That may help us." He turned to Seymour Cummings. "Which just leaves you, sir."

"And I suppose you have concocted some sort of

rationale as to why I killed Horace, have you, inspector?" said Seymour wearily. "Very well, I suppose I ought to hear it."

Andy Constable refused to be discouraged by Seymour's tone. "Actually, sir, I've got a very nice case against you. For a start, I think you're the only person who was actually heard to utter threats against Mr. Cope."

"Nonsense!" retorted Seymour. "I've done nothing of the sort!"

"Now you and I both know you did, Mr. Cummings, unless you're proposing to call Mr. Pugh a liar," said Constable. "You may not have been aware of it at the time, but the vicar was a somewhat unwilling witness to the little spat between you and Mr. Cope in the church over this new TV show that we've been told about. What is it they're going to call it – 'Seeing Stars'? And you and Mr. Cope were rivals for the very attractive job of presenter and resident clairvoyant. You were very keen to get that job, I understand. Well, who wouldn't be? I dare say there's a good deal of money and celebrity at stake. So when Horace Cope started his little campaign of dirty tricks, you were none too pleased, were you? You weren't prepared to let him stand in your way. So what we're wondering is, was that email which we've seen on Mr. Cope's computer the final straw? Did it suddenly become a matter of urgency to stop Horace Cope getting to your editor before he revealed the allegations which professionally would cut the ground from under your feet? And did you decide that the best way to stop your rival was to make Horace Cope see some stars of his own, or worse?"

"Of course I didn't," said Seymour hotly. "The idea's ridiculous."

"Sadly, not that ridiculous, sir," responded Constable. "And there might be some who would suspect that you gave yourself away with your choice of murder weapon. We're back to the final words of your altercation with Mr. Cope in church. As the vicar so delicately put it, 'Balls!'."

"But inspector!" Seymour sounded exasperated. "I wasn't anywhere near at the time."

Constable smiled. "You know, sir, it's interesting you should say that, because I've found the business of alibis in this case quite fascinating. In fact, if I were given to a belief in conspiracy theories, I should probably be coming to the

153

conclusion that I should be arresting all of you, because you're all in it together. On the face of it, everybody's movements are all accounted for, and everybody ought to have an alibi, because they were all together in the Drawing Room. Except of course that, the second you look at these alibis more closely, they all fall apart. Everybody has some time when their movements can't be accounted for. You were out in the park, sir. Miss Biding went off to get more drinks and later made a phone call, and Miss Highwater went with her. Mr. Ross went out to the Secret Garden and then went looking for you, but none of the timings dovetail precisely. Mr. Allday didn't put in an appearance until later, but there's some time we can't account for there, and Lady Lawdown was left alone for a while, and there's no proof that she remained here during that time."

"So what are you saying, inspector?" asked Sandra Lawdown. "That it was all of us? None of us? What is the point of all this?"

"I'm simply trying to explain, your ladyship, that there are almost too many threads to this case. Normally, we look at the three factors in any murder case – means, motive, and opportunity. And as I've pointed out, what is crucial here is not the motive or opportunity, because we have plenty of each. Far too many for comfort, in fact. Not to put too fine a point on it," said Constable with grim humour, "it's something of a wonder that you didn't all do it."

"So?"

"So we have to look at the means. Mr. Cope was brained with his crystal ball. Not particularly heavy, so capable of being used equally well by a man or a woman. No help there. The crystal ball has had an initial examination, and bears no fingerprints, so obviously the murderer wore gloves. And what did we find in the Secret Garden but a pair of kitchen gloves? No doubt we shall be able to get some DNA from those, and that will put this case beyond doubt. But here's a thought – Seymour Cummings told us that he re-entered the house through the kitchen, and Amelia Cook had to let him in. Amelia Cook, who has also been killed, we believe, to stop her supplying us with a crucial piece of information. I imagine she would have thought it extremely odd if Mr. Cummings, on his way through the kitchen, had made off with a pair of Marigolds.

154

"Of course, there is one other place you find marigolds, and that's in the flower room. A pair of rubber gloves is very useful for stopping your nicely manicured hands getting dirty when you're cutting flowers in the garden – or when you're up to some other kind of dirty work. And the gloves we found in the Secret Garden still have the remnants of some leaves and petals adhering to them – enough to show that the flower room is where they came from. We only know of one person who went to the flower room."

"Oh," said Sandra Lawdown breathlessly. "My lilies ..." She turned to the piano where a bouquet of lavish but drooping blooms was beginning to leave a film of pollen on the polished wood.

"Yes, your ladyship," said Constable. "Your flowers. Lilies – a symbol of death. Probably not what Horace Cope had in mind when he brought them here for you. And now those flowers are themselves dying for lack of water. Because they never did get put in a vase, did they? The vase that you went to the flower room to fetch. Didn't you, Miss Highwater?"

Helen Highwater drew herself up to face the detective. "As you say, inspector."

"But the vase never arrived, Miss Highwater. And I believe the reason to be that you didn't stay when you reached the flower room. I believe you carried on to the Secret Garden where Horace Cope was preparing for the fete. And I think you knew what you were going to do when you got there, because I think you had given up all hope of preventing Mr. Cope from destroying your greatest triumph. I think this has all been about your final Carrie Otter book. Am I right?"

An air of calm dignity seemed to settle over Helen. "Yes, inspector," she replied calmly. "You are right, of course. Horace Cope was a thoroughly unpleasant man who always knew how to twist the knife. I never knew how unpleasant he was until I heard everything that you have told us today. I believed I was alone. And I know that there is no justification for what I have done, but it makes it easier somehow to know that my friends were suffering from Horace's ... attentions too.

"And yes, it was all about my book. I dare say that sounds foolish, but my books have almost been like my children. I created them. They gave me so much unexpected

155

pleasure." She smiled faintly. "They were even going to look after me in my old age. But then Horace stepped in, just at the moment when everything seemed to come to a perfect conclusion. Just when my final book was about to be published."

"And Horace Cope somehow got hold of a copy," put in Dave Copper.

"Yes, sergeant," said Helen. "I have no idea how, and I don't suppose it much matters now. But he was intent on spoiling the whole thing for me. He said that he was planning to reveal the ending in his newspaper column the weekend before publication. I begged him not to – I asked him why he would wish to do such a thing, but I didn't get a proper answer. He just sneered. I suppose it was simply because he could. He wanted to wreck everything I have worked for over the years." She shook her head in bewilderment. "I don't understand how a person can set out to be so destructive."

"And in the end, it turned out to be self-destructive," said Constable. "In effect, Horace Cope signed his own death warrant."

"I couldn't let him do it, inspector," insisted Helen. "Not just for myself – for all my readers. All those children whose enjoyment would have been spoilt, just for the twisted pleasure of some horrible little man. So yes, I went out to the Secret Garden fully intending to put a stop to Horace and his plan. When I came through the flower room I suppose I noticed the gloves, and I think I must have picked them up almost without realising it. When I reached Horace's tent I tried one last time to persuade him to think again. Even then I gave him a chance, I really did, but it was no good. He just laughed at me and went on laying out those silly bits and pieces of his. So when I went behind him, I put the gloves on, caught hold of the crystal ball, and hit him with it. Just once. It was so odd – I felt strangely calm. And then I took off the gloves and threw them down outside and came back to the others in the Drawing Room. And I never did pick up that vase for your poor flowers, Sandra."

Sandra Lawdown moved to her friend, knelt down in front of her, and took her hands. "But Helen darling," she said gently, "I still don't understand why? Why poor Amelia?"

Suddenly, Helen Highwater's facade broke. Her face

156

crumpled, and tears began to run down her cheeks. "Oh Amelia!" she gulped. "Oh, Sandra, that was ... I wish I'd never ..."

"I think I can explain, your ladyship," said Constable. "It was all to do with the book again. Horace Cope was killed because he knew the ending and was intending to reveal it. In fact, the clue was in the title of the book itself – 'Carrie Otter and the Deadly Pillows'. And Horace Cope was overheard to boast that he knew the book's final twist. Carrie Otter dies. Horace said exactly what happens – 'she gets smothered in the end'. And that's what Amelia Cook overheard him say to Miss Highwater in the teashop. The tragedy was that Miss Cook probably had no idea of the significance of what it was that she'd overheard, but the fact that she had done so emerged during our investigations today. And I think when you knew that, Miss Highwater, you decided that Amelia's death was the only way to protect your secret."

Helen had pulled herself together. "I panicked, inspector. That is my only explanation. Once I realised that Amelia knew about Horace's words, I knew that you would understand their significance if you found out about them. So when I left the library after speaking to you, I went to the kitchen and spoke to Amelia. She was actually excited because she'd finally remembered what Horace had said that day. I realised that there wasn't any hope of persuading her that she'd remembered it wrongly, or that it didn't have anything to do with the case. I knew she would tell you, and I couldn't let that happen, so I ... well, you know what I did."

"And all so pointless, I'm afraid," replied Constable. "Because Miss Cook had written us a note. And so she ensured that she passed on to us what she knew, even though it probably seemed so trivial to her. It was the final piece to the puzzle." He paused and turned to Dave Copper. "So, sergeant, if you would ..."

Dave Copper stepped forward. "Helen Highwater, I am arresting you ..."

Andy Constable interrupted his colleague. "Outside, sergeant, I think. Miss Highwater, please."

"Of course, inspector." Helen Highwater stood and looked down at Sandra Lawdown still kneeling at her feet. "I just wish I could say how sorry ..." She turned to Laura Biding.

157

"Laura darling, look after your mother. She's going to need you." She picked up her handbag. "I'm quite ready now, sergeant. Would you like me to go first?" With a firm step, not looking backwards, she led the way into the hall.

*

As the car, driven by Sergeant Copper with Inspector Constable and Helen Highwater in the back, turned out of the rain-swept drive of Dammett Hall, it passed the now limply-drooping banner advertising the Dammett Hall Garden Fete. One of the ropes supporting the banner had come loose, and the hastily hand-written sign which had been taped to the banner had detached itself and come to rest in a puddle. Although the words were beginning to run, they were for the moment still legible - "CANCELLED DUE TO UNFORESEEN CIRCUMSTANCES".

* * * * * * * * * * * *

THE INSPECTOR CONSTABLE MURDER MYSTERIES

MURDER UNEARTHED
(First published in paperback as Juan Foot In The Grave)
A lucky win takes Constable and Copper on holiday to Spain, but murder soon rears its head among the British community on the Costa

DEATH SAILS IN THE SUNSET
Our detectives find themselves aboard a brand new cruise liner, but swiftly discover that some guilty secrets refuse to be buried at sea.

MURDER COMES TO CALL
A trio of cases for Constable and Copper to tackle - in Death By Chocolate, the victim comes to a sticky end at Wally Winker's Chocolate Factory; in The Dead Of Winter, there's first degree murder at Harde-Knox College; and in Set For Murder, there's a grisly shock in store at the Spanner House of Horror film studios.

MURDER MOST FREQUENT
Three more cases for our team of detectives – in Murder On The Rocks, they seek the killer of the owner of the Palais de Glace French restaurant; Death Waits In The Wings at the Queen's Theatre; and in Last Orders, a village inter-pub fun run takes an unexpected course.

www.rogerkeevil.co.uk

Printed in Great Britain
by Amazon